MW01137095

CRISPR
Apocalypse

A Genomic Thriller

Everything in this novel is guaranteed to happen…
timing is the only unknown…

A Novel By

Wolfgang Hunter & Anna Hasselbring

authorHOUSE®

AuthorHouse™
1663 Liberty Drive
Bloomington, IN 47403
www.authorhouse.com
Phone: 1 (800) 839-8640

Published by AuthorHouse 05/17/2018

ISBN: 978-1-5462-3716-7 (sc)
ISBN: 978-1-5462-3715-0 (e)

Disclaimers:

This is a fictional novel, written in the 2017 timeframe. The events span a period from 2016 through 2078. Every attempt has been made to ensure that the scientific facts in this book are accurate. However, the institutions, people and dialog in this account are all fictional. The names of several real people and institutions are referenced. Their words and actions are fictitious.

Acknowledgements:

We would like to thank Steve & Nancy LaMascus, Adam Hasselbring, and Alison Austin for wading through early drafts of this novel, and giving us some great advice and suggestions. We also want to thank Jose Ortega and the talented team at AuthorHouse who did such a wonderful job bringing this book to print. We couldn't have done it without all of you.

References:

References and scientific background data are available in the final pages of this book and at *www.CRISPR.guru*

CHAPTER 1

Burying Her Husband

May 20, 2078

Jane sobbed uncontrollably as she shoveled the final scoop of soil onto her husband's grave. She took a deep breath, composed herself, and slowly shuffled back to the austere concrete structure that she called home. "What is a home," she thought, "when one is completely alone?" Other than her husband, Jane hadn't seen another living soul in over two years. The earth surrounding her was a barren wasteland of death.

After securing the heavy steel door behind her, Jane walked down the steps to the bunker's lower levels. She took a seat at a large desk in the room she used as an office and began writing in her journal. Her tears dripped onto the pages, smearing the ink. It was a futile effort. No one was left to read her writings, which made her grief even more unbearable.

"I believe that I am the last person alive on the Earth" she wrote. *"This appears to be the culmination of humanity. This*

is how it all ends, exactly as T.S. Eliot predicted. Not with a bang, but with a lonely, pathetic whimper… and I am, at least partly, to blame – Dr. Jane Stewart."

She heard a noise outside. Was it the wind? A pack of wolves?

Jane put down her pen and scrambled up the steep steps of the bunker as fast as her frail 72-year-old legs would carry her. She entered the concrete structure, which was the entrance to the bunker, and grabbed her double-barrel 12-gauge shot-gun. She walked towards the small window and slowly opened the heavy blast-shutters for a glimpse outside.

CHAPTER 2

Great Grandpa Eero – Olympic Mutant

February 7, 2016

Sixty-two years earlier, a much younger Jane was still wide awake, at a very late hour.

"Come on, Jane. It's time for bed. No more stalling. Did you brush your teeth?"

"Yes, Grandma, I brushed them, but can I please watch the next *Discovery Science* episode? It's only a half hour long, and I've never seen this one before," Jane begged her Grandma Sandy.

"Don't try to pull one past me, you little uber-nerd. I know that you've seen every show on that channel a dozen times, and it's already *way* past your bedtime. Your mom and dad are going to have a cow if they find out that I let you stay up this late."

"Okay," replied Jane in defeat. "But can you tell me a bedtime story? Maybe one about Great Grandpa Eero?"

Grandma Sandy sighed, "Fine, but only if you get your little butt into bed right now!"

Jane smiled, turned off the TV and ran into her room. She quickly slid under the covers. Shortly thereafter, Grandma Sandy joined her and pulled a chair next to her bed.

Other than her issues with going to bed on time, Jane was a spectacular kid, especially for a ten-year-old. She was doing great in school, she had plenty of friends, and she was fascinated with science, particularly biology. Whether it be TV shows, documentaries, library books, websites, or online lectures designed for people three times her age, she had an incredible thirst for knowledge.

Jane's affinity for science was appreciated by her Grandma Sandy, who was a retired genetic biologist. Sandy and her husband, Al, had moved to Washington, D.C. a few years earlier to be closer to their son Adam and his wife Ellen, who were both high-ranking executives in the U.S. Government. The couple's busy schedule gave Sandy plenty of one-on-one time with her beloved granddaughter, Jane.

Grandma Sandy and Jane said their prayers. Then Sandy started another tale about the family's legendary Great-Grandpa Eero.

"Way back in the 1960s, when I was a little kid like you, my dad, Eero Mäntyranta was the greatest cross country skier that the world had ever known."

"That's back when you lived in Finland, right Grandma?"

"That's right. We lived in the city of Pello, and your Great-Grandpa Eero skied for Finland's national team. He won four world championships and seven Olympic medals. I remember watching him compete and cheering for him in the 1964 Winter Olympics at Seefeld. He was amazing. He completely blew away the competition! They called him 'Mr. Seefeld' because it seemed like every Olympic highlight-reel featured him." Grandma Sandy's eyes welled up a bit as she reminisced about her father, who had passed away fifteen years earlier. She turned away briefly to wipe her tears, then regained her composure and continued the story.

"I was so proud of him! I cheered as loud as my voice would carry. I told everyone in the crowd around me that the skier way out in front of everyone else was my daddy!"

"I'm going to be a world champion when I grow up too, Grandma," interjected Jane. "Then you can be proud of me and tell everyone, 'Look at that girl out in the lead! That's my granddaughter Jane! Isn't she awesome?'"

Sandy leaned over and gave her granddaughter a kiss on her forehead.

"Jane, I am already very proud of you, and I will always be. No matter what great things you do when you grow up -- which I'm sure will be many."

"I'm already the fastest runner in my class! Yesterday, in PE, we raced three times around the playground and I beat everyone, even the boys. I wasn't tired at all!" Jane beamed with pride, as did Grandma Sandy.

"Well, Jane, let me give you a little biology lesson. When you breathe in, the oxygen in the air goes into your lungs, and then your red blood cells carry that oxygen from your lungs to your muscles, right?"

"Yep", answered Jane. "And then those red blood cells carry the carbon dioxide from your muscles back to your lungs. And then your lungs breathe the carbon dioxide out, to get rid of it."

Grandma Sandy smiled, "I might be biased, but you're a pretty smart little kid."

Jane flipped her hair with pride.

Grandma Sandy continued, "In our bodies there's a protein called erythropoietin, or EPO. EPO's job is to regulate the production of those red blood cells. The more EPO you have, the more red blood cells you will have in your bloodstream."

"So, Great Grandpa Eero must have had lots of red blood cells, right?"

"Yes, he did. Years later they tested him and found that he had a mutation in his EPO receptor gene which increased his red blood-cell count by 50%".

"He had a mutation?" asked Jane, a bit shocked. "You mean like mutants and zombies? I thought that mutations were bad."

Grandma Sandy laughed, "No, Jane. *'Mutant'* just means *'different'*. Sometimes gene mutations are good, sometimes they, are bad, and most times mutations don't seem to do much of anything. I was never tested because I had already moved to America, but scientists from the University of Helsinki did test my brothers, sisters, and cousins over in Finland. They found that most of my relatives had the same EPO receptor gene-mutation as my dad."

"Is that why I can beat everyone in my class? Because I'm a mutant like Great-Grandpa Eero?" Jane's face looked a bit worried and confused.

Grandma Sandy smiled and gave Jane a quick hug. Maybe she had stuffed a tad too much information into this bedtime story, even for her precocious little grand-daughter.

"You may have the EPO mutation, or maybe you're just insanely fast for some other reason. In any case, you probably shouldn't tell your classmates that you might be a *mutant*. That may not go over so well."

Jane's brow furrowed as it did every time that her brain churned with ideas and questions. "So, why can't scientists give everyone this EPO mutation? That way *everyone* could be fast!"

"Well, some athletes have taken EPO to boost their red blood cells, but that's considered cheating."

Jane looked perplexed, "How is that cheating? Wouldn't letting other people increase their red blood cell levels just even things up?"

"Have you heard of Lance Armstrong?"

"The guy who rides bikes and wears tight yellow clothes?"

"That's him! He was one of the most highly-decorated racing cyclists in the world. He used artificial EPO to get the same advantage that your great-grandpa had naturally. However, because Lance's EPO was synthetic, he had to return all of his gold medals, and he was stripped of all his titles."

"Woah!" exclaimed Jane. Her little head was now spinning with ideas. "So, Grandma, what if, instead of *taking* EPO, a smart scientist like you designed something that tricked a person's body into *making* more of its own EPO? That wouldn't be synthetic, so it wouldn't be cheating, right?"

Jane was obviously just trying to put off going to sleep as long as possible, and Grandma Sandy took the bait. "Well, I did read about a group of scientists who are working on an injectable virus which is designed burrow into a person's cells and modify the EPO receptor gene in a way that would allow that person's body to make far more EPO. Those researchers are primarily trying to help people who are sick, but I suppose that those same treatments could be used to help athletes as well."

"See Grandma. *That* would make things fair. That way we *all* could be great athletes, just like your daddy!"

Grandma Sandy wasn't so sure about that. In any case, she wasn't going to let Jane delay bed-time any longer.

"That may or may not be a good idea, Jane," replied Grandma Sandy. "But right now it's time for this little smarty-pants-athlete to close her eyes and get some sleep."

Jane sighed and laid back down. Grandma Sandy tucked her into bed, gave her a kiss on the forehead, and walked towards the doorway.

"Goodnight, Grandma. I love you!"

"I love you more," replied Grandma Sandy as she turned out the light and closed the bedroom door behind her.

"No, Grandma, I love you a million billion times more!" giggled Jane.

Grandma Sandy smiled and shook her head in the hallway, "Go to sleep Jane."

CHAPTER 3

Alarm Bells in the U.S. Senate

February 7, 2016

The reason that Grandma Sandy was babysitting little Jane was because Jane's dad, Adam Stewart, the United States' Deputy Director of National Intelligence, was working late, yet again. While his daughter, Jane, was skillfully avoiding bedtime, Adam was walking briskly through a hallway in the basement of the U.S. Senate building with his boss, James Clapper, the Director of National Intelligence, and John Brennan, the Director of the CIA.

Adam and the two directors were heading to a classified meeting with both the House and Senate Select Committees on Intelligence. The purpose of this joint meeting was to review the direst threats to the security of the United States. These findings would then be used to define funding priorities for the Department of Defense and other government agencies. The meeting was referred to as the *Annual Worldwide Threat Assessment Hearing*.

Adam and the directors had already supported public briefings for both the Senate and the House earlier in the week. Those open-meetings, which had been broadcasted to the world via C-SPAN, were, frankly, of little value. They were primarily used to placate the civilian population and, in some cases, to intentionally spread misinformation to America's enemies for national security purposes.

The real work of the government was performed in closed, top-secret, Special Access Required (SAR) meetings, like the one being held on this night. In a highly-secured room, in the basement of the Senate building, Adam, Director Clapper, and Director Brennan greeted the congressmen from the Joint Committees, and took their seats.

The room was a Sensitive Compartmented Information Facility (SCIF), a secure location for cleared personnel to hold secret meetings. There were strict rules for the meeting attendees. Cell phones and personal computers were prohibited. Attendees could bring pens and paper, but all notes were confiscated at the end of the meeting and locked in the SCIF's enormous document safe. The SCIF was accessed via a hallway with three successive sets of thick steel doors, only one of which could be opened at a time. This provided the SCIF with physical security and prevented any radio signals from escaping the SCIF.

Director Clapper kicked-off the briefing: "It's well known that Americans face many threats, from many foes. In the past, we've testified regarding traditional terrorism, cyberattacks, nuclear proliferation, and threats to our power grid. Today, however, a new threat will be the focus of our briefing. This is a totally new potential Weapon of Mass Destruction. A WMD which could be far more destructive than any weapon this world has ever experienced. It is called *CRISPR.*"

The congressmen and women fidgeted in their chairs, unnerved by Director Clapper's urgency regarding this strange new threat.

Adam stood and continued with his portion of the classified briefing. "CRISPR is a new genetic editing tool. It is the most incredible invention in the field of genetic science to date. It could be the key to eliminating all cancer in our lifetime. Its positive impacts for the medical community will be immeasurable. On the other hand, CRISPR also has the clear potential to be used as a WMD. The deliberate or even unintentional misuse of CRISPR could lead to far-reaching economic and national security implications."

Senator Brian Landgraf, a medical doctor by training, interrupted. "Hold on, Adam. There are already hundreds of genetic biotech tools on the market; those tools have been around for decades. Why are you so concerned about this CRISPR tool?"

"Yes," replied Adam, as he paced nervously in front of the congressmen. "Hundreds of genetic editing tools have been developed over the past few decades. And CRISPR is the only one that has ever been included in our threat assessment. Previous tools were very expensive, and complicated to use. This made it easier for us to control their proliferation and minimize their use. But CRISPR is very different, and far more dangerous. We believe that CRISPR now ranks above all previous threats, including

North Korea's ongoing nuclear tests; China's enhanced nuclear capabilities with the establishment of its so-called *Rocket Force*; Russia's development of its *ZIRCON* hypersonic cruise missile, which clearly violates multiple treaties; and even Iran breaking the Joint Comprehensive Plan of Action by restarting its nuclear development efforts."

Adam tried to make eye contact with each committee member in the room, striving to emphasize the seriousness of the issue.

"The key problem is that CRISPR is dual-use. As Director Clapper pointed out, CRISPR could be used to cure almost any human ailment. On the other hand, it could be used to create a killer mosquito, or a plague that could wipe out crops. Or terrorists could create a virus that kills humans by sniping-out crucial segments of people's DNA, at the molecular level."

Adam took a seat as Director Clapper continued the briefing, "We are also concerned about how other countries will utilize CRISPR..."

Senator Landgraf interrupted, "Not just countries. I heard that Sean Parker is already funding CRISPR trials right here in America."

Senator Julie Valleroy's interest was suddenly perked, "Sean Parker? The Napster guy? Wasn't he played by Justin Timberlake in that *Facebook* movie?"

"Exactly," responded Director Clapper. "Even someone like Sean Parker, who has virtually no background in genetic biotechnology, can be a major player in this CRISPR-god game virtually overnight. But we are particularly worried about the CRISPR research which is being conducted by countries with far less-stringent regulatory and ethical standards than ours. This could easily result -- intentionally or unintentionally -- in the creation of an unlimited assortment of harmful biological agents."

Adam chimed in, "For instance, China just announced that they have used CRISPR on human embryos to correct a gene that causes a blood disorder. At Sichuan University, they are using CRISPR techniques to treat lung cancer. Both of which sound great, right? But it's a slippery slope."

Director Clapper interjected, "It's worth pointing out that, this year, at the *International Summit on Human Gene Editing*, all of the countries in attendance agreed that CRISPR-modified cells should not be used to establish a pregnancy."

"But they didn't implement a *legal* ban," Adam countered, "It was more like a suggestion, or a recommendation. And, even if they did implement a ban, how would it ever be enforced?"

Senator Landgraf rejoined the conversation. "A year or two ago, we had a hearing with Francis Collins, the director of the National Institute of Health. He told us back then that the NIH would never fund gene-editing technologies for use in human embryos."

"That is correct," replied Adam, "but that was eighteen months ago, before CRISPR techniques had proliferated. Back then, scientists needed millions of NIH dollars to edit genes. Now you, me, or any terrorist wannabe, can go online and order a CRISPR gene-editing kit for a couple hundred dollars, sometimes as low as $60."

Director Clapper added, "The Cas9 enzyme, which the CRISPR uses, is truly sensational. It's essentially, a pair of molecular scissors with an embedded map of exactly where a specific DNA molecule needs to be cut. The Cas9 enzyme uses a hunk of RNA which is precisely encoded to guide those scissors right to the designated section of DNA which needs to be removed. Once that existing gene sequence is eliminated, it's relatively easy to replace the deleted section of DNA with a new re-engineered string of atoms. The Yunnan laboratory in Kunming, China, is using CRISPR to create Macaque monkeys with purple eyes, orange eyes, any color that they want. And eye color is only the start. There may be no limit to the genetic modifications that this technology can perform."

Clapper paused to take a drink from his water bottle and resumed his testimony. "Even scarier, there is now a new version of CRISPR called Cpf1. For many applications, it's even more powerful than the traditional CRISPR Cas9. Cpf1 requires only a single RNA, which further simplifies the process, and it has a staggered cleavage pattern which recognizes thymidine-rich DNA sequences, whereas Cas9 mostly recognize guanosine-rich sequences. In layman's terms, Cpf1 greatly broadens both the scope and the precision of CRISPR editing. Frankly, it's terrifying."

"The most daunting and possibly catastrophic thing about CRISPR is that it's not just a one-time event." Adam continued pacing in front of the group of legislators. "When a bomb goes off in a city – bam – that's it. There might be fatalities, or injuries, or destruction, or PTSD, but, for the most part, the damage is done. The mayhem is contained to one area. On the other hand, when a gene is modified in a plant, animal, or a person, you do *not* contain the modification to that one living thing. The mutation can be inherited, not just by their direct offspring, but also by their children's children. CRISPR technology can genetically alter every future generation, to the end of the species."

Representative Emeric O'Dell from Louisiana shook his head, "Gentlemen, I have only comprehended about one-third of what y'all have said this evening, but I do know that y'all have sufficiently scared the crap out of me. You have *not*, however, answered the billion-dollar question. Hell, it's probably more like a hundred-billion-dollar question." The representative eyed Adam, Brennan and Clapper. "That question is: What are those of us in this room supposed to do to clean up this huge pile of hog feces that y'all have dumped upon us this fine evening? We've funded programs to address all your other threats – North Korea, ISIS, whatever. What the hell are we supposed to do with this one?"

Adam, Brennan, and Clapper looked at each other, each hoping that one of the others would deliver the bad news. Finally, Director Clapper took a deep breath, moved a bit closer to his microphone, and answered. "Representative O'Dell, to be blunt, the genie is out of the bottle. CRISPR is everywhere, and anyone with $100 in their wallet can buy a kit. If we outlaw CRISPR-kit manufacturing here in the America, it will just move overseas."

Adam Stewart tried to help his boss, "Sir, frankly, most of the CRISPR kit manufacturers are already overseas. If we had caught this thing two years ago, we *might* have been able to make the technology classified and stopped…"

Director Clapper interrupted, "Even if we had taken draconian measures two years ago, we wouldn't have *stopped* anything. We might have delayed CRISPR for a couple years, maybe for a decade, that's it. At this point, I'm not sure that there is anything we can do to stop it."

CHAPTER 4

Genes, and DNA, and Chromosomes – Oh My

September 9, 2021

"OK, class! Quiet, please. That was the bell. It's time to start today's lesson. That's better. First things first, can anyone tell me what a *paramecium* is?" Ms. Jones stood in front of the pool of sophomores, who were now gawking at her in a dazed state of confusion.

"Anyone? No? Alright, then you better write this down. A paramecium is two Latin mice! Get it? A *pair-of-mecium*?" Ms. Jones keeled over at her desk, laughing hysterically, as her students groaned in embarrassment at her geeky taste in humor.

"I'm sorry. Science jokes just don't get much better than that, kids."

16-year-old Jane Stewart sat in the third row of Ms. Jones' biology class, her favorite subject of the day. Over the years, Jane's fascination with science had only grown

16

stronger, as her knowledge expanded exponentially. Today, however, Mark Simpson, Affton High's soccer star, who had the attention span of a gnat, was sitting directly across the aisle from Jane. Unfortunately, that sweet hunk of eye-candy was making it difficult for Jane to give her full attention to the lecture.

Ms. Jones quickly segued into the day's lesson. "Does anyone have questions about your reading assignment from last night? Chapter 4, pages 112 through 138? You all read it, right?"

A room full of blank stares was an obvious sign that virtually no one, other than Jane, had bothered to read anything. So, Ms. Jones proceeded to lecture the material that the students should have read the previous evening. Ms. Jones was a spectacular teacher. Unfortunately, thirty minutes into the period, most of the class, and especially Mark, appeared to be totally lost. So, Jane decided to assist Ms. Jones, Mark, and the rest of the class, by asking a simple question.

"Miss Jones, I know that you've explained this to us before, but what exactly is the difference between genes, DNA, and chromosomes?"

"Good question, Jane. I'll try to make it simple."

"Like Biology for Dummies, man. That's what I need, ya know?" added Mark.

Ms. Jones couldn't help smiling. That boy was dimmer than a black tar roof at midnight, but he sure was a cutie. *If I were just a decade or two younger*, she thought…

Miss Jones quickly cleared her mind of those marginally inappropriate thoughts, and got back to teaching. "As you all know, DNA is the genetic material that defines each unique individual. DNA is an abbreviation for 'Deoxyribonucleic acid'... Don't worry, you won't be tested on that."

"Perfect! I will forget that fact *immediately*," exclaimed Mark.

"What I meant to say was that the full name isn't important. You *will* need to know how DNA works, so please, try to pay attention Mr. Simpson." Miss Jones walked to the board and wrote:

Genes → DNA → Chromosomes

"The simplest way to think about the relationship is that a gene is a section of DNA. Human DNA is made up of around 25,000 genes. A chromosome is a package which holds a DNA molecule. The long DNA string is folded thousands of times and wadded-up to fit inside a chromosome. This folding is very important. A straight, unfolded DNA molecule, for instance, would be far too large to fit inside of a cell. And those chromosome packages are then bent into various shapes.

"In biology, the shape of a molecule can be very important, especially when it comes to DNA and proteins. Two proteins that are chemically identical, for instance, can have vastly different effects on the body depending on how they are folded. If a protein folds one way it can be harmless, but folded another way can cause diseases, like Alzheimer's or Mad Cow disease."

Mark spoke up, "My uncle had cows... One of them was sort of mad... I'd say that it was more *angry* than mad... Just a really mean, angry old cow..."

"OK, Mark. Thanks for that contribution. Not overly relevant. Maybe raise your hand next time?"

"Got it, Ms. J."

"The structure of DNA was discovered by two guys named Watson and Crick back in 1953. A DNA molecule looks like a twisted ladder, it's called a double helix. The rungs of the ladder are called 'base pairs' and those are the keys to all life on Earth. There are four components of base pairs: Adenine, Guanine, Thymine and Cytosine".

And with that, Miss Jones lost the attention of the entire class. Their eyes glazed over. Mark hung his head in surrender, his long blonde hair covering his gorgeous eyes. Miss Jones and Jane both glanced over at him and gave a wistful sigh.

"OK. Don't worry about that. No one uses those names in the real world anyway. Each of those rungs -- Adenine, Guanine, Thymine and Cytosine – we refer to them by their initials: A, G, T and C. Four letters! That's all you really need to remember. Those four letters are the keys to life."

Mark's head bopped back up.

"AggggTuck!" he shouted, startling the entire class.

"Excuse me?" queried Miss Jones.

"AggggTuck... A-G-T-C spells AggggTuck. I can remember that. OK, I've learned one biology-thing today. That's my quota Ms. J. I can't overload my brain with too much stuff or all the knowledge just starts falling out the other side, ya know?"

"That's nice, Mark. Today, however, I think that we can extend your learning quota just a bit further. Those strings of letters, *AggggTuck* as Mr. Simpson has so creatively named them for us, make up the rungs of DNA's molecular 'ladder'. Something like CATCGCTGC for instance. Those strings of letters are the 'words' that tell our bodies what to do. They make our eyes blue, our hair thick, or whatever."

The girls in the class, and two of the guys as well, glanced over at Mark, wondering what magical strings of genes had created those awesome eyes, hair, and all his other parts. Meanwhile, Mark stared out the window and wondered why school busses were yellow.

Ms. Jones continued. "A gene is just a segment of DNA. Some genes are made up of only a few hundred 'letter pairs', while others consist of two million letter pairs, or 'rungs', on the DNA ladder".

Ms. Jones glanced around the room. She hadn't *totally* lost them yet...

"Human DNA has around 25,000 genes, packed into three billion rungs."

Ms. Jones looked into the eyes of her students, trying to determine if any of this was sinking in. Grasping these basic concepts was crucial if any of them were going to make an impact in the field of genetics. That was her goal, to inspire just one or two of her students to go out and do great things. Was that too much to ask?

"When you were conceived, your unique DNA was created by choosing one of each of those 25,000 human genes. In each case, your DNA molecule could choose the gene-string from your mom, or the gene-string from your dad. In most cases, it didn't matter, because most genes are identical in all humans. The genes that differ, the 'variable genes', are called *alleles*. The allele genes determine if you are short or tall, left-handed or right-handed, or, in some cases if you are healthy or sick."

Jane's hand shot up again, "But how does the DNA tell your body what to do?"

Ms. Jones strutted back to the front of the class, shaking her finger at the sky as she often did when she got excited. Because *this*, at least to her, was some *very* exciting stuff.

"That, my dear students – *that* subject gets a little more complicated. Let me try to make it very simple."

"Inside your cells, the codes in the DNA molecule (AGT&C) do two amazing things: Replication and Transcription. Both Replication and Transcription occur because the DNA components (AGT&C) chemically want to 'pair up' with each other in certain ways.

"Replication is the ability of DNA to constantly create an *exact* copy of itself. DNA molecules are constantly replicating themselves.

"DNA replication occurs because adenine (A) pairs with thymine (T), cytosine (C) pairs with guanine (G), and, conversely, thymine pairs with adenine and guanine pairs with cytosine.

"However, the most important talent of DNA is called *transcription*, which is DNA's ability to create a *different* string-like molecule called RNA. RNA transcription works just like DNA replication, except that the base uracil (U) replaces thymine (T).

"RNA molecules are primarily used to create various types of proteins by stringing together thousands of amino acid units".

Jane's hand shot up again. "What's an amino acid?"

"And why should I care?" groaned Mark.

"Amino acids are important because they create proteins. Proteins are huge molecular strings of amino acids. The human body needs about 100,000 different types of proteins to live. These 100,000 proteins perform many different tasks, from growing various types of tissue to fighting disease and even transporting other molecules to the correct spots in our bodies. Proteins are created by RNA -- and RNA is created by DNA – and that's the magic that creates…"

The bell rang, and interrupted Ms. Jones mid-sentence.

"Your projects are due on Thursday and we are going to have a quiz on Friday! Study now! Don't wait until the night before the quiz!..."

Ms. Jones watched distractedly as Mark Simpson sauntered towards the door. She wondered if anything that she had said in the past 45 minutes had sunk-in.

"Bye, Ms. Jones."

"Goodbye, Jane. Have a great day."

"You too!"

CHAPTER 5

Some Help from Dad

September 9, 2021

The world has seen many revolutions over the centuries. The Babylonians revolted against the Assyrian Empire in 626 BC. Spartacus led his slave revolution against the Roman Empire in 72 BC. The French and American Revolutions both rocked the concept of royalty in the late 1700's. These were all world-changing events. They all, however, paled in comparison to the CRISPR revolution.

Jane came home from volleyball practice to a delightful surprise; her father was home before dinner time! She sprinted into his office and gave him a big hug from behind his office chair.

"Hello stranger!" Jane squealed as she wrapped her arms around her father's neck while he sat at his desk, typing away on his laptop.

"Hey kiddo! How was practice?"

"Same old, same old" Jane replied. "Why are *you* home already? The sun is still up!"

"My boss let me take-off early today since I had to work last weekend and missed my daughter's birthday."

"And yet, here you are, holed up in your office."

"Sorry honey. I just can't unplug. There are some nasty threats out there. Even at night I find myself dreaming about this crap."

"Well, Mr. Deputy Director of National Intelligence. Is there any top-secret info that you can enlighten me with?"

"Actually, a lot of the really scary stuff is *not* classified." Adam handed a news article to Jane. The headline read: *Zageno Labs Reports Record High Sales of CRISPR Kits.*

"I remember you talking about this. CRISPR is a new genetic editing tool. Right?"

"Yep. I've spent the last five years of my career trying to control the proliferation of CRISPR, but it's been unstoppable."

Jane skimmed the article. "This is cool stuff, Dad. Do you need any certification or a license to buy one of these bad boys?"

"Unfortunately, no. Ordering is so simple, it's scary. You just go to *www.Zageno.com*, or any other on-line CRISPR supply shop, and place your order from a user-friendly menu of options." Adam logged onto the web-site to show Jane how it worked.

"You start by choosing a gene of interest from this menu of options. Then you choose the gene-effect desired; for example, which gene to knock-in or knock out, or both knock-in and knock out. Then you choose the DNA 'break type', which can be double strand or single strand. And, finally, you choose the new genetic fill material."

"It's that simple?"

"That's it! If you have a problem, you just call the 1-800 number at the bottom of the page. A friendly customer-service agent will help you find the perfect combination of CRISPR gene-editing tools to bring you mutant-creating dreams to reality. It's petrifying."

"Wow. It must be expensive, right?"

Adam shook his head. "Old editing methods, like recombinant DNA, TALEN, and the strangely named *Zinc Fingers*, those were all *very* expensive. CRISPR, on the other hand, is dirt cheap. Those old technologies are now as useless as buggy-whips on a Ferrari."

Jane was intrigued. "Why do they call it CRISPR?"

Adam laughed. "CRISPR is an acronym for Clustered Regularly Interspaced Short Palindromic Repeats. The term doesn't make any sense because CRISPR was discovered by accident. The CRISPR molecule was found because it was messing up other tests. Originally, it was the name of a problem, not a solution."

"It's amazing how many discoveries seem to happen by accident."

"Two different teams stumbled on CRISPR at around the same time. One group was from Germany and Berkeley, and the other was from Harvard, MIT, and a smattering of loosely-aligned biotech firms. Once they finally grasped the power of what they had accidently discovered, they all spent the next decade suing the pants off each other. As usual, only the lawyers got rich."

"You know Dad, you did miss my birthday last weekend." Jane raised her eyebrows and gave her father a big smile. "Showing me how to use this CRISPR gene-editing tool would be a great belated birthday present!"

Adam laughed. Only his daughter would ask for such a goofy birthday present.

"Please, Dad? This is the stuff I live for!"

"Why can't you just ask for a car like a normal 16-year-old?"

"You know, Dad, if Grandma was still around, she'd be stoked to hear that I was interested in gene editing."

Adam reminisced about his beloved mother who had passed away earlier that year from Alzheimer's. The crippling disease had horribly deteriorated his mother's once incredible memory, her sanity and her health. Who was he to stop his daughter from possibly helping others, as she wished she could have helped her grandma?

Adam sighed and handed over his credit card, "On one condition. You log all your work religiously, and by no means will you ever experiment on any animal. Not even a flea."

"Yes, dad. I promise!"

Jane gave her dad another big hug and ran out of his office, but then skidded to a stop and popped her head back through the door. "Just for the record, Dad, you are more than welcome to buy me a car too. Any color is fine, as long as it's pink."

Over the next few years, Jane experimented with CRISPR technology for hours on end, often with the help of her father. It was soon clear that Jane had an uncanny knack for determining optimal knock ins and knock outs to achieve a desired genetic result. Jane's fascination with CRISPR, and her passion for science, continued to grow.

CHAPTER 6

Zika, Malaria, and Gene Drive

July 12, 2023

Jane graduated from Affton High School as her class' valedictorian, among other honors. She was awarded several more-than-full-ride scholarships, including one to Arizona State University, so money wasn't an issue. Her future was extremely bright.

Although Jane didn't really have to work during the summer between high school and college, she figured she'd keep herself busy by accepting a paid internship at Genotek LTD, assisting an eccentric staff scientist named Rick Rostek. Her position was supposed to be mostly grunt-work, cleaning the lab and fetching coffee, but Rick quickly recognized Jane's scientific savvy and decided to utilize her brain for more important tasks.

"I just don't get it" declared Rick as he stared into his microscope at a mosquito larvae.

"OK, I'll play along," replied Jane. "What don't you get this time, Doctor Rick?"

"Don't get me wrong, I'm grateful to the anonymous rich guy who gave us this grant to investigate mosquitoes, but it's insane that we even need to do this research. In the 1800's and early 1900's Malaria used to kill millions of people every year. And then, around 1939, we nearly wiped it out -- virtually eliminated malaria from the face of the Earth, with DDT. It was a *wonderful* chemical, so safe that humans could actually eat it by the spoonful with no harm…"

Jane laughed. "I wouldn't say with *no* harm. But, yes, I've seen those *YouTube* videos of people eating DDT with no *apparent* ill effects."

Rick disregarded Jane's comment and continued his rant. "Then, in 1962, that crazy novelist, Rachel Carson, writes a junk-science-filled piece of fiction called *Silent Spring,* and scares the crap out of everyone. She got everyone to believe that DDT would give people cancer, and that it was wiping birds off the face of the earth. Next thing you know, DDT is outlawed, malaria returns with a vengeance, and in no time, we are back to having millions of new human infections and half a million-people dying from malaria every damn year!"

Jane smiled. Dr. Rick was definitely a few cards short of a full deck, but she found his passionate tirades to be quite amusing. "It does seem crazy that we're getting paid to use something as little-understood as genetic engineering to combat Zika and Malaria, but we're not allowed to use a well-understood, proven-safe chemical like DDT. On the other hand, it's funding my summer paycheck so I'm not complaining."

Rick wasn't quite done. "I'm sure that Rachel Carson's intentions were pure. She probably meant no harm, but the cold hard fact is that, through her book, she may have indirectly, caused the deaths of more people than any other single person in human history. Tens of millions, maybe as many as fifty-million deaths."

"That's a little harsh, but I guess it's a fair point."

"Yes! It's a spectacular point! Because I made it, and I'm freakin' brilliant!" Dr. Rick exclaimed while laughing. "But I've had quite enough of your goofing around, Jane. Back to business! Are you making any progress on your third-generation gene-drive mosquito mutation?"

"I'm getting really close. The one that I created today looks like it may work. First generation reproduction is spectacular, second generation reproduction is spectacular, and then nothing."

"Cool. That's exactly what we need." Rick patted Jane on the back and returned to his microscope.

Genetic traits are usually inherited by the next generation, from either the father or the mother, at an equal rate of around 50% from each. If you draw an "ancestry tree", you will see that, in most cases, if one person in a population has a certain altered gene (aka a mutant gene), it will never spread too widely through a population from one generation to the next, unless, for some reason, there is a lot of in-breeding.

But, in nature, some genes have a trait that is called Gene-drive. This is a relatively rare phenomenon in which a genetic trait gets inherited at a rate significantly higher than 50%. Sometimes these are called *"selfish genes"*.

If a gene is engineered to be *"selfish"*, with a gene-drive of 55%, or even 99%, then, over a few generations, that gene's trait will spread rapidly throughout a population.

Back in 2021, scientists at the University of California Irvine (UCI) had used CRISPR to edit the genes of a mosquito larva to prevent it from transmitting malaria. Then they added gene-drive, which allowed that trait to spread throughout the mosquito population.

Rick and Jane's goal was a bit different. They wanted to use gene-drive to engineer sterility in mosquitoes carrying diseases such as malaria or ZIKA. This is a little trickier than what the researchers had done at UCI.

Even with a spectacular tool like CRISPR, engineering sterility in a population is no walk in the park. Creating a single sterile lifeform is easy, sterile animals occur all the time. The problem is that a sterile individual does not result in a sterile population because that one sterile individual, *by definition,* does not reproduce. When the sterile individual dies, the gene that made him/her sterile dies with it and that sterility problem is removed from the gene pool.

To create a sterile *population*, you first need a gene that is very prolific – the exact opposite of a sterile gene. You need a gene, modified with gene drive, that reproduces like wildfire and spreads throughout a given population. And *then*, after that gene has spread prolifically, it needs to, somehow, become a sterile gene, which makes the entire population sterile. It's complicated, but, if it works, it is very powerful.

CHAPTER 7

Genetic Engineering Didn't Start with CRISPR

Humans have been practicing genetic engineering for tens of thousands of years, long before they had any real understanding of what genes or DNA even were. Before DNA was discovered, genetic engineering was referred to as botany (for plants) or animal husbandry (as it related to creatures).

Pre-CRISPR, brute-force genetic engineering, by selective breeding, was very effective. It changed some populations by as much as thirty standard deviations in only a few decades. Domestic chickens, for example, have increased in size by 400% since the 1950's.

Genetic tinkering has massively improved life on earth, at least for humans. Genetically re-engineered crops have virtually eliminated world hunger. Today, in third world countries, where starvation was rampant back in the 1960's, obesity is now a much larger problem than starvation, even where population densities are now three times what they were when hunger was common. In the 1960s, the overwhelming scientific consensus was that *most* of the world's population would be starving by the year 2010. It's amazing how often "scientific consensus" and "settled science" is later proven to be absolutely wrong, eclipsed by new technology, or even social-political events.

By the 2020s, however, CRISPR changed the game forever. Not only was CRISPR much easier, faster and cheaper, CRISPR was also the equivalent of a rifle-shot vs a blast of shotgun pellets – a laser-guided micro-missile verses indiscriminate Dresden-like carpet-bombing.

Later, other CRISPR editing advancements which allowed researchers to modify base pairs one at a time, without the need for cutting, was even more exciting. This method was ideal for correcting so-called point mutations, where only one base pair in a DNA molecule required modification.

Then, a tool called CRISPR CAS13 was developed which enabled the precise editing of RNA. With CAS13, rather than trying to create a DNA molecule that would create the desired RNA modification, the RNA molecule could be edited directly. This gave scientists even more control over the keys to life.

CHAPTER 8

It Isn't Easy Being Green

June 9, 2024

After completing her freshman year at Arizona State University, 19-year-old Jane was thrilled to learn that she had landed a summer internship with GreenFuel LTD. Not yet knowing exactly what she wanted to be when she grew up, Jane was pursuing a double-major in both genetics and mechanical engineering. She envisioned herself combining those degrees into a career in bio-medical engineering, maybe inventing genetic medical tools and devices.

GreenFuel Ltd was a small company. Their business involved interbreeding various types of algae. Their ultimate goal was to create a new strain of algae which would produce an oil that could be refined into gasoline and diesel fuel. The oil-producing-algae had to grow at an incredible rate when placed in water-filled glass tubes, infused with carbon dioxide, and then exposed to sunlight in the desert. This idea had been an unfulfilled dream of environmentalists for decades. The theory was that, not only would the algae produce fuel directly from sunlight, it could also consume voracious amounts of that evil greenhouse gas, carbon dioxide (CO_2), fed to it, via pipeline, from traditional coal-fired or gas-fired power plants.

On Jane's first day at GreenFuel she was paired with George West, GreenFuel's chief scientist. George met Jane in the company's sparsely-appointed lobby,

"Welcome to GreenFuel. I assume that you are Jane, our new intern?"

"Yes, sir. It's a pleasure to meet you." she replied.

"Nice to meet you too, Jane. I'm George. You and I are going to be playing with slime for the next three months."

"Looking forward to it, sir."

As an intern, Jane got stuck doing all the jobs that George didn't want to do. She would breed the algae, growing it on a plate in the lab's *Phenometrics* photo-bio-reactor. Then Jane would test samples from various points on the plate to evaluate the quality of the oil that the algae produced. Finally, she would re-breed only those algae samples which produced a slightly higher-quality oil than the previous "best of breed". Breeding algae was a messy, smelly, somewhat boring job, but Jane didn't care. She was learning new things every day.

One Friday afternoon, two weeks into her internship, Jane was having a sandwich with George in GreenFuel's small lunch-room.

"How are things going, Jane? Are you sick of working with green-goop yet?" asked George.

"Absolutely not. This is great. And I just got my first paycheck yesterday, which makes me happier than an F5 ripping through a trailer park."

"To each their own I suppose." George took a bite of his salad and continued his questioning, "How are your samples performing?"

"Well, I guess that they're getting a little better every day, but this sure is a slow way to do it."

GreenFuel was doing genetic engineering the old way, by selective evolution. It was a snail's-paced process which relied on capturing random genetic changes to eventually create a better algae.

"Genetic evolution takes time, Jane. Even when you're playing God by doing intelligent selection."

"So, why not do active genetic engineering instead?" asked Jane.

George scoffed. "Been there, done that. Way too expensive, not nearly precise enough."

Jane's superior was not only a Scrooge, but, for a trained scientist, he was also quite the luddite. George displayed absolutely no desire to adopt new methods or to alter his ways. But Jane, always the optimist, was convinced that she could shake him out of his old habits and make some huge leaps forward.

"Have you tried CRISPR Cas9?"

"I've heard of it."

"Well, I've used CRISPR a lot" replied Jane, "both at ASU and on my own. It's dirt-cheap, its precision is outstanding, and it's far faster than the way we are doing it now."

"I'm rather fond of doing things the old fashion way," replied George, with a sense of pride and assurance.

"No kidding, Captain Obvious" thought Jane, straining to avoid speaking her thoughts aloud.

"How much are we talking about?" asked George. "I was lucky to scam enough budget to pay for your salary this summer. Money is tight around here."

"We wouldn't need much. Probably less than 200 total."

George scoffed. "No way in hell that you can execute an active genetic engineering project for two hundred-thousand dollars. Maybe for ten times that much if you're lucky."

Jane laughed. "No, George… Not 200 thousand… or for 2 million. Just two hundred dollars. Like two Benjamins. If your budget is really that tight, then I can just buy a kit myself. If this idea works, you can pay me back with stock options, or whatever."

George wasn't sure how to respond. He sat in total silence for a spell, just staring at the cafeteria wall behind Jane. Then he rose from his chair, grumbled something like, "Keep pluggin' away, kid", and shuffled out of the lunch room, back to his office.

Jane immediately chose to interpret George's less-than-enthusiastic reaction as management's unmitigated approval of her idea!

That Friday night, while GreenFuel's other interns were using their fake IDs at the local bar, Jane spent her evening defining the exact genetic splices that she believed would transform GreenFuel's present algae-strain into an optimized, fuel-generating organism, on steroids.

By 4 am on Saturday morning Jane had all her genetic "knock-outs" and "knock-ins" defined. She filled out the on-line form for a CRISPR-kit that would perform those exact DNA manipulations, and sent it off to www.Zageno. com, along with her personal credit card number. $169 for the kit, plus a $30 rush charge to ensure that an Amazon drone would deliver it to her apartment by 9am Monday morning. As the sun began peeking over the horizon at 5 am, Jane's head finally hit the pillow…

"You're late," complained George, pointing dramatically at his watch as Jane sauntered into the lab at 10:03 on Monday morning with a cardboard box tucked under her right arm.

"Sorry, George. But, if this works, I think that you'll forgive me for being a little late."

"What's in the damn box?" asked George, tilting his head to read the blue lettering on the side of the carton. "And what the hell is a 'Zageno'?"

"This is a CRISPR kit, George. We talked about this on Friday? You approved it, remember?"

George raised his eyebrows, "I don't remember approving nothin'!"

"George, if this works, eight hours from now, that sour-puss face of yours is going to be grinning like a horsefly nibbling on a cow-pie."

"OK…."

"George, we are going to create an algae strain that not only produces the sweetest, lightest, most refinable crude oil the world has ever seen, we're also going to design it to reproduce four times faster than the most virulent strain you've created to date. I think that I've picked a set of gene modifications that will deliver every one of those characteristics."

George scoffed, "In your dreams, newbie! Squeezing all of those characteristics into a single strain of algae is impossible."

Over the next eight hours Jane showed George how to implant her newly-created CRISPR-virus molecules into the algae spores. Once implanted, the CRISPR molecules began slicing and dicing the spore's DNA to create the precise genetic characteristics that Jane had envisioned.

When exposed to the right conditions of temperature, moister, food and light, those genetically-engineered super-spores germinated and quickly grew into adult algae cells. Those algae cells then produced more spores, but those new spores didn't have to be genetically altered. They had already inherited all the genetic enhancements that Jane had previously given to that asexual spore's mother/father spore. And the mutant reproduction process repeated itself over and over again.

By the end of the day, the lab was producing ever-increasing volumes of Jane's new strain of mutant-algae, just as she had predicted. Breathlessly, George stared as tiny droplets of bioengineered algae trickled up to the top of the photo-bio-reactor, where it formed a lighter-than-water film. He skimmed off a sample of the new mutant-algae and tested the oil that it produced. It was an oil of spectacular quality.

George rocked back in his chair in amazement. The oil was almost identical to Texas light sweet crude, which is the best, most easily refinable crude in the world. Not only could Jane's version of algae-oil be refined into gasoline, diesel, and jet fuel, using *existing* refineries and processes, it could also replace all the other uses of crude oil. It could be used as a feed-stock to produce plastics, nylon, polyester, and thousands of other materials that were presently made from crude.

"Not bad, rookie." George said with a smile. He no longer even noticed the putrid aroma of algae permeating his lab. The stench had been transformed, at least in George's mind, into the sweet smell of money.

CHAPTER 9

Chimeras

<u>***December 19, 2024***</u>

Per Greek mythology, a Chimera is an amazing fire-breathing monster. It sports the body of a goat, the head of a lion, and the tail of a snake. The Chimera is an impressive cocktail of a beast. In Greek lore, the Chimera finally meets its demise at the hands of Bellerophontids, the son of Poseidon, who kills the Chimera while riding his legendary winged-horse, Pegasus. That story is a spectacular myth. CRISPR-created Chimeras proved themselves to be quite the formable beasts as well. But they were *very* real.

In the early 2000's, diabetes was one of the leading causes of disability and death in the United States. Many of the symptoms were treatable, but the only real *cure* for diabetes was a pancreas transplant. The problem was that the pancreas had to be a near-perfect match to the recipient. And it had to be taken from a relatively healthy donor who was physically alive, but, hopefully, brain dead. As a result, very few people who needed a new pancreas ever received one before meeting their maker.

During the winter break of her sophomore year, Jane's father twisted some arms to get her an internship with his old friend, Dr. Walter Hightower, a professor of neurosurgery at the University of Minnesota. It was a typically frigid December afternoon in Minneapolis as Walter sat in his office chatting with Jane. Dr. Hightower was explaining the intricacies of the mundane, yet vital, task of writing NIH grant-requests to keep his lab funded for the next semester or two. Walter hated this part of his job. Jane, however, thought that it sounded fun. She gladly volunteered to take-on the assignment of writing his grant requests.

Walter had lost his brother and several other relatives to a variety of organ diseases. Many of his relatives could have been saved with timely transplants, but all had died before organs had become available. Those losses had motivated Walter to dedicate his professional life to fighting organ disease – pancreatic diseases in particular.

Walter was explaining some of the goals and objectives of his lab to Jane. "As you probably know, pigs are, at least biologically, very similar to humans. This should, in theory, make them excellent *biological incubators* for human organs."

Jane nodded, "So, you want to create pig-human chimeras?"

"Correct. The idea of creating chimeras isn't new. Scientists have already created a mouse with a rat's pancreas, and even a mouse whose liver was made from human-like liver tissue. I, however, believe that far more is possible, especially if we use CRISPR tools. That's why your dad suggested that I hire you as an intern. By using CRISPR, I hope that we can grow not only human pancreases inside of pigs, but other human organs as well."

Jane looked up from her notes and responded, "I know that with human-to-human transplants, rejection is always a huge problem. Chimera-grown organs, done correctly, should fix that problem. Right?"

"Yes, the chimera-created organs will, in theory, be a perfect match to the patient, so rejection will no longer be an issue. The first step is to harvest some of the patient's induced Pluripotent Stem (iPS) cells which can be taken directly from the patient's failing organ, a pancreas for instance. Those organ stem cells are then combined with a pig embryo which is then implanted into a female pig. The resulting piglet will contain a nearly-perfect, but, of course, younger and healthier copy of that human's own organ. This perfect-match means that anti-rejection drugs -- which often create as many problems as the transplant itself -- can be greatly reduced, or even eliminated.

"Our problem at the moment is getting the pig embryo to accept the human iPS cell's DNA. That's where you come in, Jane. With your CRISPR experience, and your knack for gene editing, I'm hoping that you can figure out some way to make my chimera-dream a reality."

Jane scrunched her face as she pondered the problem. "Sure," she said. "To grow a human pancreas in a pig, first we will have to delete all of the pancreas gene sequences from the pig's DNA. I can do that using some tailored CRISPR tools. Then we just need to fill those genetic holes with *human* pancreas genes, which we could harvest from the iPS cells using other CRISPR molecules."

Over the next four weeks, Jane cranked out six grant-requests to the NIH. In each, she explained various portions of her chimera pig / CRISPR / iPS / pancreas transplant ideas in excruciating detail. Amazingly, all six proposals were enthusiastically accepted and fully funded by the NIH. Over the next six months, the University had to triple the size of Walter's labs. Walter was absolutely thrilled and begged Jane to stick around to help him execute the work. By then, however, Jane was already back in the warmth of the desert sun, acing her grueling 26-hour course-load at ASU with ease.

CHAPTER 10

Tubes in the Desert

June 2, 2025

Despite getting A's in all her classes, certain aspects of Jane's sophomore year had been rather stressful. The algae-loving slime-balls at GreenFuel had reneged on their verbal agreement to give her stock options in return for her CRISPR-enabled super-algae creation. As she continued her studies at ASU, GreenFuel's stock had soared, but Jane received nothing. Her supervisor, George, had claimed that Jane's mutant algae was solely his idea. George received a plethora of stock options which made him an extremely wealthy man, at least on paper.

Eventually, the truth leaked-out that Jane had been the real brains behind the discovery. Even without the full recognition she deserved, Jane was building a resounding reputation as a genetic scientist, and was actively courted by several companies to intern with them during the summer between her sophomore and junior year.

One of the companies courting her was *SwitchYeast Inc.* They wanted to use Jane's CRISPR-skills to create a new type of yeast that would break-down Switch Grass into ethanol.

Traditionally, ethanol has been produced from corn. Corn is much easier to refine into ethanol than Switch Grass, but corn requires copious amounts of water. Back in the 1990's the environmental and farm lobbies had convinced the U.S. government to require the addition of corn-based-ethanol into gasoline. This artificial demand forced farmers to grow corn in dry areas, which, in turn, required huge amounts of irrigation. Most of this water was extracted from the massive Ogallala aquifer, which underlies the U.S. Great Plains, from West Texas to Eastern Wyoming. All of this excessive irrigation had contributed to the Ogallala's near-depletion.

Switch Grass, on the other hand, could produce more ethanol per acre than corn, but with only one third the water. It was the perfect answer. Unfortunately, there was no efficient process to break-down Switch Grass into sugar and ethanol. Designing a CRISPR-modified yeast that could break it down was the obvious answer, which was exactly what the company aptly named *SwitchYeast* wanted Jane to invent for them. Jane was certain that she could have solved that DNA riddle. This summer, however, she wanted to try her hand at something completely different. A totally new industry -- a company called *KrystalTube,* whose business had virtually no relation to genetics.

Jane was melting in the summer heat. Her boots were half buried in the scorching sand dunes of southern New Mexico, just south of White Sands Missile Range. She was brainstorming fixes for her project's latest series of problems with Felix Cooper, a business major from the University of San Diego, who was also interning at KrystalTube that summer.

Felix wiped the sweat and sand from his brow and shook his head, "Jane, you're absolutely nuts. I can't believe that you turned down an internship doing your genetics crap, in an air-conditioned lab, for a hideous construction job out here in the middle of 'hell'".

"This may not be hell, but I think I can see it from here," quipped Jane. "And I hate to be the bearer of bad news, California beach-boy, but you haven't even felt *hot* yet. It's only early June. Just wait until August. Living in hell is paradise compared to White Sands in late summer." Jane glanced at the construction equipment surrounding them, none of which appeared to be doing much of anything. "How are things going so far today, Felix?"

"Typical. We're FUBAR'ed already, same as yesterday and the day before that. We've had three tube-trucks arrive so far. Two are stuck in the sand, the third finally made it out to the site, only for us to discover that the tube had cracked somewhere between here and the factory. It's just screw up after screw up."

"Was the crack reparable?"

"Hell no. It was a total loss. It had to be scrapped."

Jane sighed, "This is insane. We need to fix this mess."

The algae that Jane had invented the year before at GreenFuel was spectacular. It was a key piece of the total puzzle. But that piece was somewhat useless until all the other pieces were in place as well. The next element to tackle was building and installing thousands of miles of glass tubing out in the desert to grow the massive amounts of algae required to satisfy the world's thirst for oil. This is why Jane chose to spend her next internship with KrystalTube Inc.

Felix shrugged his shoulders in defeat, "Or we could just go home early, crack open a cold beer, and call it a day."

Jane smiled and rolled her eyes at Felix. With his constant complaining and blatant desire to avoid anything resembling work, she wondered how he had ever been hired, even as an intern. She figured that he must be a relative of someone in *KrystalTube's* executive suites. Jane, on the other hand, hated just complaining about problems. She also despised *managing around* problems. She was fanatical about engineering permanent solutions to the glitches she found around her.

"So, one problem is that the tubes keep breaking during transit. Another is that it's costing us a fortune to build roads over the sand to allow the trucks to haul the tubes out into the desert," Jane stated.

Felix chimed in, "And the glass tubes can only be 45 feet long to fit on the trailers. Which means that we need to install joints every 45 feet. That's 117 joints per mile. Each of those joints need to be sealed, and when they leak, we have to pay battalions of insanely expensive laborers to march out into this hideous desert heat to fix those leaks."

Jane pondered their dilemma. "Elon Musk likes to talk about 'machines that produce machines'. Cavemen first produced utensils and weapons, but that didn't make them much better than other animals. Birds build nests, beavers build dams, and apes throw rocks and feces at their enemies. The real progress came when cavemen started creating machines that could build other machines. First, it was a simple tool, like a hammer, made from a stick with a rock tied on the end. Eventually it will be robots designing and building other robots. Creating, not just exact clones of themselves, but engineering improvements to make every robot generation more capable."

Felix frowned, "And then, humans will no longer be needed?"

Jane shook her head. "That's what some people think. But it doesn't keep me up at night. Progress has always been about using automation to eliminate people's jobs. In the early 1800s over half of all Americans worked in agriculture, now it's less than 2%. Which means that roughly half of the U.S. population lost their jobs to agricultural automation."

"Yes, but that was a good thing. It got people out of the fields and into better jobs."

"That's how you see it today, but that's not how those unemployed farm workers saw it back in the day. Farm skills were all that they had. Farming was their life."

Felix scoffed.

"Felix. Your last name is Cooper, right?"

Felix was wary, "Yeah, so, what about it?"

"Do you know what Cooper means?"

Felix was a bit befuddled. "No… But it's a popular name, so it probably means something."

"In old-English, Cooper means 'bucket maker'. Centuries ago, every village had a Cooper who made buckets. It required years of training and apprenticeships. A cooper would take several days to fabricate a single wooden bucket.

But a good Cooper could sell his buckets for a week's wages or more. Today, however, the market for $1,000 custom-made wooden buckets has evaporated. We can now buy a far superior plastic bucket -- made in a highly-automated Indonesian bucket factory -- at Walmart for a couple bucks. The key question is: *Is this a bad thing, or a good thing?*"

Felix pondered Jane's question as the red-hot sand blew directly into his scorched eyeballs. "I guess that it's a bad thing for us Coopers, but it's a good thing for everyone else?"

"I've seen your construction skills, Felix. You can barely swing a hammer. I am pretty sure that your future family would starve to death if they had to rely on your ability to fabricate wooden buckets by hand for their survival."

"They wouldn't last a week!" replied Felix as he pointed to the scrap-pile in the distance. "But how do wooden buckets from the 1700's relate to that enormous pile of overpriced, broken glass tubes?"

"Well Felix, I am sick of wasting my summer sitting here watching everything break around us. What if we develop a way to make this process so efficient that we put virtually everyone in this god-forsaken desert out of a job? The truck drivers, the assemblers, even the people back at the tube factory? What if, instead of trying to build a machine that makes algae, we invent a machine that *builds* a machine that makes algae?"

"Ooookay, and how do you plan to do that?" Felix asked.

Jane reached into her briefcase, and pulled out a notebook filled with drawings.

"This is such a cool idea," she giggled. "So, the way that we use robots today is sort of like cheating. The robots are usually just blindly assembling parts that humans give them. And they do everything in a nice clean factory which makes for a sterile and controlled atmosphere. But that's very different from how humans and all other living creatures operate. Our bodies organically reproduce and maintain ourselves. We extract all the raw resources that we need from the environment around us. I want to use that same concept for this project."

Jane pointed to her drawings. On the paper was a sketch of some sort of a machine, crawling through the desert. It had a forest of Fresnel lenses, mirrors and solar panels suspended above it, and a glass tube trailing behind it like an infinitely long tail.

Jane continued. "Instead of building glass tubes in a factory, and then hauling them out here into the desert, this machine will crawl through the desert using the energy from sunlight to gather the quartz sand around it. The robot will then purify the sand, melt it into molten glass, and form it into four-foot diameter, *continuous* glass tubes."

"Continuous? So, there won't be leaky joints every 45 feet?"

"None."

"No roads required? No stuck trucks? No tubes broken in transit?"

"Nope." Jane smiled. "This invention eliminates every major problem that we currently have, and it cuts labor costs virtually to zero. The machine digs a trench for the tube to lie in, and then uses the sand from the trench to make the glass for the tube. The machine is solar-powered. We have plenty of sun out here, so we don't have to haul fuel out to the crawler. It's totally self-sufficient."

"Do you really think that you can collect enough solar energy to melt glass?" Felix asked.

"That is one of the tricky parts. The sun only projects around 1,000 watts per square meter of energy onto the Earth. Standard photoelectric solar panels waste around 85% of that solar energy. For a heat-intensive process like melting glass, the key is to use curved mirrors and Fresnel lenses to guide and amplify nearly *all* of the sun's energy directly onto the purified quartz sand. In this case, I am using one hundred square meters of mirrors and Fresnel lenses to precisely focus, one hundred-thousand watts of solar energy onto a very small volume of sand, which is quickly pre-heated to around 2,300 degrees Fahrenheit. Then, ten solar-powered CO_2 LASERs will be used to liquefy the purified sand into glass by raising its temperature to just over 3,000 degrees Fahrenheit, one cubic centimeter at a time. Rather than melting hundreds of pounds of glass and forming it into a tube, the tube will be built from the desert sand by a continuous process of melting and adding glass to edge of the tube."

"Sort of like additive manufacturing or stereo lithography?"

"Exactly. But on a massive scale."

"What if the sun doesn't shine? What if the crawler breaks down?"

"A maintenance team could ride quads or sand-rails through the desert to check on the crawler if a repair is needed. And the crawler will have a satellite phone to call for help as required."

"Having a Sat-phone is a definite requirement. Because, as we all know, there is no damn cell-phone coverage out here in the middle of hell." Felix grumbled as he glared at his bar-free iPhone.

"The crawler will have limited back-up battery power. But when there's no sun, the crawler will just shut down until the sun returns."

Felix paged through Jane's drawings and equations. "This is a pretty cool concept, Jane. Are you going to show it to management?"

"I have a 30-minute meeting with the head-shed next week."

"You're not going to use these crappy drawings, are you?"

Jane hesitated, "Well… Yes?"

Felix laughed. "OK, Jane. I may not be nearly as smart as you. And I definitely can't build a wooden bucket like my highly skilled forefathers, but I am a business major and I know how to create a killer business plan. Let me help you blow these suits away."

For the remainder of the week, and right through the weekend, Jane and Felix spent every spare second perfecting their pitch for a crawler that would revolutionized the algae-tube fabrication business. Their compelling business plan was a huge hit, and the executives immediately implemented Jane's novel idea. In mere months, prototype versions of Jane's crawlers were covering the desert floor with algae-growing glass tubes. KrystalTube's stock quadrupled, but this time Jane was well-rewarded. She and Felix were both given extremely lucrative stock option packages. Those options eventually turned Jane and Felix -- into millionaires, many times over.

CHAPTER 11

The Work-a-holic or Sloth Gene

Late 2025

It had been a crazy six months. The executives at KrystalTube had richly incentivized Jane and Felix to skip their fall semester to stay at KrystalTube for an additional five months -- through the end of the year.

Things had changed in other ways as well. A summer of working 60 or more hours every week, had cumulated in a surprise "appreciation dinner" for Jane and Felix with their bosses, including KrystalTube's CEO, Ben McCleary, and his wife Holly. Jane and Felix were treated to speeches praising their contributions to KrystalTube, including a seven-course meal consisting of filet mignon, lobster, and more than a few bottles of Dom Perignon. That night, Felix somehow ended up in Jane's hotel room and a few weeks later he moved into her apartment. It was a decision that seemed to make sense at the time. After a few months of shacking up, however, it was clear that the bloom was off the rose – not that there ever had been much of either a bloom or a rose in this couple's dysfunctional relationship.

As usual, Jane had rolled out of bed at 4am, worked-out like an Olympic athlete for forty-five minutes, and arrived at work by 5:30am. At 11:45am she was absolutely starving, so she ran back to her apartment to grab lunch -- half of a day-old Subway foot-long -- left-over from last night's dinner. Even though Jane was now a multi-millionaire, she still hated the idea of wasting anything. As she flew by the master bedroom, she saw Felix, still lying in bed under a muddle of sheets and bedspreads.

Jane skidded to a stop. She could feel the steam blasting from her ears.

"Felix Cooper! It's almost noon. Get your lazy ass out of bed!"

"Just fifteen more minutes!" whined Felix.

Jane shook her head in disgust. "Don't you have any motivation? Or dignity? Or an ounce of shame? Dammit, Felix. It doesn't matter how much you've done for KrystalTube, if you don't even bother to show up at your desk, you're going to lose your damn job. And, by the way, you still owe me $900 for your share of last month's rent and utilities!"

"Please, woman! You know that I have the money to pay you. And, I'm sorry that I'm not a crazy, psycho, work-a-holic like you. Jesus, woman, get off my back!"

Jane shot back. "You really want to go all Nazarene on me, atheist boy? I'll tell you what Jesus thinks. Second Thessalonians, chapter three, verse ten! *He who does not work shall not eat!*"

"Really? Well here's my quote: *'Hard work pays off in the future; but laziness pays off today'* – so turn your ass around and take it out through the in-door because I may decide to stay in my bed all freakin' day long!"

His outburst complete, Felix pulled the covers over his head.

Jane had never laid in bed until the crack of noon her entire life. At least not since she was an infant. In a few rare cases, if she was sick, or extremely hungover, she *might* get crazy and lay in bed until 8:00am, but anything later than that was utter madness.

Jane had had enough. "Actually, sir, this is *my* bed!" she exclaimed as she yanked the blankets off of Felix's extraordinarily sedentary body, and threw them onto the floor. "So, if you don't want to be a functioning member of society, then you really need find a new bed where you can waste your life away -- by yourself."

"Your loss, babe." Felix sauntered out of bed, strolled into the master bathroom, slammed the door shut, and locked it behind him. Jane grabbed her left-overs, stomped out of the apartment, and slammed that door behind her for good measure before driving back to the office.

Jane and Felix's relationship had gone quite well in the beginning, but their differing views on work-ethic had become an obstacle that neither of them seemed able or willing navigate around.

Jane devoured what was left of her sandwich at her desk as she scanned some recently released papers on genetic research. A paper on the PER1, PER2 and PER3 genes caught her eye. All three of these so-called 'period homolog genes' helped regulate circadian rhythms in humans, the internal clock, so to speak, that keeps the human body's sleep patterns in sync with the sun.

The PER3 gene especially peaked her interest. She saw that recent research indicated PER3 may be a "Work-a-holic or Sloth" gene. The article indicated that variations in the PER3 gene could be the difference between people who seem to be constantly productive versus those, for example, who prefer to lay in bed until noon. PER3 also seemed to determine a person's response to alcohol and stress. PER3 gene production varied widely from person to person, by at least a factor of 500%. The paper also inferred that PER3 may regulate other down-stream genes which were already known to control behavior.

Jane was 99% certain that she would be removing Felix from her life permanently. As she finished her lunch, however, she scribbled down a note to herself to test Felix's PER3 gene levels, in the off-chance that she ever changed her mind about kicking his ass to the curb.

CHAPTER 12

Free Money

December 22, 2025

Jane was responding to emails when a head popped into her cube and interrupted her train of thought.

"Jane, we're having a meeting and we would like to hear your input."

It was Kris Shackleford, KrystalTube's V.P. of Finance. Jane shut her laptop and followed Kris into KrystalTube's executive conference room. The room was filled with V.P.'s and Directors. Jane knew about half of them, but they all seemed to know her. Jane's inventions had made them all extremely wealthy.

Taylor Aiton, KrystalTube's Vice President of Research kicked off the questioning.

"Jane, we need your advice. The U.S. Department of Energy and DARPA have both offered us grants which could be worth over $80 million. They want to give us money to accelerate our investments in algae-tube and crawler production. Frankly, we've always been a private-sector company and we have no experience with government grants, but this one sounds too good to pass up. We know that you have worked on government-sponsored programs in your previous jobs, and that your mom and dad are both high ranking government officials, so we wanted to see if you had any ideas to help us grab this funding."

Jane quickly paged through the two sole-source Requests For Proposals (RFPs). She frowned and shook her head.

"Why on earth do you want to do this? Why would you let the U.S. government into your boy-shorts?"

The group of good ole boys sitting around the conference table were a bit befuddled. "It's $80 million, Jane. It's free money. That's why!"

"No, it's not free at all. You'll have to deal with a gaggle of U.S. Government bureaucrats. They will slow your progress to a crawl… and that's not just a pun because we're in the crawler business." Jane's lame attempt at humor fell flat, so she continued. "In the end, the government will try to claim that they own *all* of your designs even though they paid for only a tiny fraction of the development."

Taylor Aiton begged to differ. "Jane, your major is in genetics, right?"

"Well, yes. Mechanical Engineering and Genetics."

"How about that whole sequencing of the Human Genome thing back in the '90s? That was a huge government program, right?

Jane threw her hands up in the air. "Right! And how the hell did that work out?"

"It worked out great."

"No, it didn't! It was a stupendous waste of money. The government-funded DNA mapping study was beat like a rug by a tiny upstart private company named Celera Genomics. Celera started their *privately-funded* sequencing effort several years *after* the U.S. government started theirs. But Celera's tiny team still completed their mapping long *before* the massive government team completed theirs."

"I didn't know that."

"Of course, you didn't. Because the U.S. Government and their lemming-like minions in the press buried the story. Celera's mini-team was led by Dr. Craig Venter. Since they had no government '*help*', to drag-down their efforts, Craig's team not only moved faster, but they sequenced the human genome for *ten times less money* than the government team."

Taylor Aiton shook his head. "OK, that's one example, but it's an outlier. I'm sure there are plenty of other instances where government funding has been beneficial."

Jane was on a roll. "No, it's *not* an outlier. Take manned flight as another example. Between 1895 and 1903 the U.S. Government spent today's equivalent of hundreds of millions of dollars funding Charles Langley and others to invent the first airplane. The government didn't give a dime to the Wright brothers, but Orville and Wilbur were the first to fly by a long-shot! More importantly, in the years that followed, the Wright brothers were also far more successful building and selling airplanes than any of their government-sucking competitors."

The executives in the KrystalTube conference room stared at 'Jane the Intern' in stunned disbelief.

"So," stammered Kris. "I guess this means that we *shouldn't* accept the government's offer of grant money?"

Jane smiled. "Gentlemen, that is totally up to you. But if this were my company, I'd run away from those RFPs faster than an ice cream truck being chased by Melissa McCarthy."

The executives mumbled amongst themselves.

Jane smiled. "Is that all you needed from me?"

There was more mumbling around the table

"Alrighty then. I'll just mosey on back to my tiny little intern cubical. You all have a great day. And again Mr. Aiton, as I mentioned last week, could you please send that letter to my advisor at ASU so she doesn't think that I've just been goofing around all semester?"

CHAPTER 13

The Beauty Gene

April 22, 2026

It had been four months since Jane left her extended internship at KrystalTube and resumed her studies at ASU in Tempe, Arizona. But even with her new-found wealth, and growing status in the scientific community, she remained well grounded and totally focused. More importantly, she was thoroughly enjoying her return to college-life.

It was a gorgeous Saturday evening. Jane and her roommate Cindy Murray were primping and preening for a night-out on the town, but getting there was turning into even more of a production than usual.

"Jane! Hurry up, I would really like to get to *Mill Ave* before last call," yelled Cindy.

"I look hideous!" Jane screamed from the master bathroom.

Cindy ran over to find Jane staring into the mirror, analyzing her face intently.

"Oh please, you look great! Now let's go!"

Jane turned to look at her stunning blonde-haired, blue-eyed friend and sighed. Then Jane turned back to the mirror and applied yet another layer of contour, in a futile attempt to chisel her rather lame cheek bones.

"Cindy, humans may be 99% genetically identical, but your 1% is far superior to mine. You can just roll out of bed and still manage to get every guy's number in the entire bar. But *this* face right here, this mess requires some major work. I'm going to need you to be a bit more patient."

Cindy laughed. "Jane, you are nuts. It's not like that at all. Now, let's go!"

Jane ignored her friend and babbled on, as she grabbed an eyeshadow palette from her makeup bag. "Fun fact, scientists are now certain that all of you blue-eyed humans have a common ancestor. Seven thousand years ago, a fisherman on the banks of the Black Sea had a spontaneous molecular genetic 'defect' which gave him, you, Frank Sinatra, and all his other decedents, those hypnotic blue retinas that make every cute guy in the bar want to dance with you all night long, instead of me! For that genetic-lottery loss on my part, yes, I am more than a little bitter."

"Oh, thank God for another genetic fun fact! That's *exactly* what I need to get me psyched for a long night of heavy drinking."

"Speaking of fun facts, I read today that researchers just found two copies of a gene on chromosome number two that code for a protein called Myostatin – you know, like "muscle halt".

"Huh?" replied Cindy.

"Didn't you go to Catholic grade school? Didn't those sadistic nuns beat Latin into your brain? *Myo* is Latin for 'muscle' and *statin* means 'halt'"

"No, Jane. The sisters failed miserably. Five years of Roman Catholic Latin classes and I do not remember even a single word. But, apparently, you are a master of useless dead languages, so, if we meet any Roman Centurions in the bar tonight, if we ever actually get there, you will be in luck! So, let's go!"

Jane was unphased. "Remember that super baby in Germany? He was amazing. He was six months old and had zero bodyfat. He could do an iron cross on the rings when he was one. Apparently, he had a mutation where, not just one, but both of his *Myostatin*-producing genes were turned off, so his muscle production was *never* halted. He just kept getting stronger and stronger. Wouldn't *that* be an incredibily cool mutation to have?"

"Oh, yes, Jane. That would be so *Fetch!* But do you know what would be even cooler? If we could get to the damn club before it closes!"

Jane admired Cindy's sense of humor and her fiery attitude. Although she was a bit more laid-back than Jane, Cindy, an advertising major, was also a work-a-holic in her own right. Jane also loved the fact that Cindy was willing to tolerate her ramblings, no matter how annoying or relentless they might be.

Since kicking Felix to the curb, Jane had been reluctant to go out on a limb and start dating again. It wasn't that she was irreversibly tainted by the experience, but it had taught her that she had certain standards, a few bare minimums that she was looking for in a man. And she never wanted to settle for less.

"Honestly Jane, aren't you being a bit over-dramatic about your looks? Plenty of guys are attracted to you, you're just too damn picky to give them a chance."

"That's probably fair, but, *whatever*. Back to *my* point!" Jane continued the monologue that always accompanied her endless makeup-application sessions. "A person's eye color is determined by the pigment in a part of the iris called the stroma. But, there is no such thing as *blue* stroma pigment! Blue eyes actually occur when there is little or no pigment in the stroma. The gene that's responsible for blue eyes is called OCA2, and it also controls melanin. Prior to that one Black Sea fisherman with those mutant blue eyes, all humans had brown eyes. His particular mutation limited the OCA2 gene's ability to produce melanin in the iris, and, *Voila!* blue eyed-people were soon spreading all over the planet, ruining weekends for those of us who are cursed with normal, non-mutant eyeballs."

"Riveting stuff, Jane. I'm sure the frat boys will be enthralled with your tantalizing scientific information."

Jane would not be rushed. "And another thing my blonde-haired, blue-eyed, nemesis… The genetic mutation that codes for your naturally stunning golden locks was also recently identified. It was found in a gene sequence called KITLG. The blonde mutation, in that string, is present in about one-third of the residents of Northern Europe. A tiny tweak of only one letter in the KITLG genetic code can ramp-up or ramp-down the production of pigment in the hair follicle which determines hair color…"

Cindy looked down at her phone, no longer feeding into her roommate's incessant nerd-rant. "I'm ordering a car."

"It's not clear why blonde hair was so important. It could be that those blonde-hair genes also produce light-skin, which helped ancient humans in the frozen north survive in the dismal, dreary, low-light conditions of that region. Light skin would have also resulted in the production of more vitamin D, which is crucial to survival."

"Again, *so* interesting. Please wrap it up so we can leave!"

Jane stared at the mirror pulling at her face to get a better angle, trying to glob as much mascara onto her eyelashes as they could possibly hold.

"I need to just glue on some false lashes. I can't deal with my wimpy lashes right now." Jane rummaged through her vanity drawers like a whirling dervish.

"Are you kidding me? Jane, I'm going to kill you. Your eyelashes are beautiful just the way they are."

Jane looked over at her gorgeous friend's eyes. "No, *your* eyelashes are beautiful! You must have three times as many eyelash hairs as the average person, it's fascinating."

Cindy was exasperated, "I think we have two very different definitions of the term fascinating, because you are seriously killing my buzz."

Jane looked at herself in the mirror. "Fine. I guess that this will have to do!"

Cindy's phone chimed, "Good, because Omar Abu is outside in his charcoal gray Nissan Sentra to pick us up."

As much as Jane's dear friend Cindy may have been less than amused by the science behind her lashes, there were plenty of other people who were interested in having them. It turns out that she had a genetic mutation called a

Distichiasis transcription. Distichiasis transcriptions were one of the first beauty-type mutations that the human gene-editing industry would offer. It was marketed as the "double eye lash" enhancement. Using CRISPR technology, scientists edited a few key DNA genes on the sixteenth chromosome. This simple edit caused people to grow a second row of dark, thick, spectacular eyelashes, just like Cindy's.

In the decade between 2030 and 2040, nearly one billion women -- and a couple million men -- received this double eye lash gene therapy, giving themselves the same genetic mutation that Cindy had obtained naturally via the genetic lottery.

CHAPTER 14

A Party Foul

April 22, 2026

The music was blasting at *El Hefe* in Tempe, Arizona. Jane, Cindy, and six of their closest friends were having a spectacular time drinking, dancing, and laughing until they were sore. It was well after midnight, and the girls were plenty liquored up.

Several groups of young men were sitting at the bottle-service tables, desperately attempting to impress the women in the club with the number of sparklers featured in and around their massively over-priced bottles of liquor. Jane hadn't computed her net worth lately, but it was probably in the neighborhood of $70 million. It certainly exceeded the net worth of all the male patrons in *El Hefe*, and the two clubs next-door, combined.

Obviously, Jane could easily have afforded a bottle service table for her and her friends, but she viewed the bottle service concept to be utterly stupid. Instead, Jane and her friends spent most of their time dancing and buying rounds of drinks the old fashion way, at the bar, or from the wandering waitresses. Jane always picked up the majority of the tab, even though her inebriated friends fought like cats and dogs to split the bill with her.

"I don't care how much money you have, Jane. You shouldn't be buying us drinks! That's what God made guys for!" yelled Cindy over the DJ's blaring techno-remix. Jane couldn't comprehend why her comrades were so irresistibly drawn to those swarms of men and their sparklers. They resembled schools of Red Snapper circling a shiny lure, but they were definitely having fun, swinging by the tables, making new 'friends', and occasionally flirting with the bottle-service-boys, while consuming a free shot -- or three -- in the process. This whole scene was nowhere near the top of Jane's lists of favorite things to do, but she was happy to play along. "I'll only be this young once", she thought. Jane recalled a favorite quote of her father's: *"Most people who are old and wise, got that way by first being young and rather stupid"*.

Cindy's head snapped around to a table behind Jane, "Oh! Look! That table has a couple bottles of Medea Vodka!"

Jane looked at her friend in puzzled disbelief. "That stuff is horrible! I get a hangover just looking at it."

"Fair enough, but I love the way the words on the electronic label scroll around the bottle... It's hypnotic -- like watching a Zamboni. And, the guy at the head of the table is *really* hot, so we need to make some compromises! OK?" Cindy gave Jane a devilish grin, "Be my wing-girl?"

"Cindy! I'm already way too drunk. I am *not* in the mood to charm some random bros right now."

"*Charm?* What are you? An English noblewoman from the seventeenth century? Come on! It's only one drink. Please?"

Cindy gave her best friend a big boo-boo lip.

Jane sighed and shrugged her shoulders in defeat. Cindy squealed with excitement, grabbed Jane's hand, and drug her friend across the dance floor to the bottle-service table.

"Hello, boys! Mind if we join you?" Cindy asked flirtatiously, while leaning over to show-off her lowcut dress.

"Absolutely, come-on up!" responded the hot guy that she had been eyeing, who was now practically drooling at the site of this beautiful blonde climbing into his table.

Jane noticed a hand reaching out, offering to help hoist her into the booth. She grabbed it and looked up.

"Well, look who it is!" exclaimed Felix, as he pulled Jane into the table.

"Just when I thought this night couldn't get any better," responded Jane, sarcastically, while giving the evil-eye to her best friend, Cindy, from across the table. Not that Cindy even noticed. She was already fully preoccupied with her new prospect.

"It's great to see you too, Jane," replied Felix.

Jane and her ex-boyfriend hadn't seen each other since breaking up and going back to their respective universities. They had fought like cats and dogs while living together in New Mexico, but in the end, they had separated on somewhat friendly terms. Even though their personalities were as different as night-and-day, the fact that they had made their first fortunes together would always be a unique bond between them.

"What're you doing in Tempe, Felix?"

"Visiting some friends. And I'm getting interviewed for that *30 under 30* thing with *Fortune Magazine* in a couple days. Of course, you will probably be on the cover, with a lead article, and I'll just be mentioned in the bowels of the magazine with the also-rans."

Jane smiled as Felix handed her a shot. "You're looking good, Felix."

"Cheers!" he replied as they clinked glasses and slammed their respective drinks. "You know, Jane. I hate to admit it, but you may have had a valid point when we broke up."

Jane raised her eyebrows inquisitively, "Really?"

"Yeah. I actually took *some* of your words to heart. I now am working out at the crack of dawn, *almost* every day, my grades are better than ever, and I'm on the boards of a few businesses that I invested in."

"That's awesome!"

"Not that you *totally* broke me. I still enjoy the occasional 'stay in bed and binge on Netflix all day' – but now, it's only every week or two, instead of every day or two!"

"You do love your shows!" Jane laughed while trying to wash away the taste of that last shot with a hefty gulp of her fruity cocktail.

Jane was still certain, regardless of any changes that Felix may have made, that the two of them were *never* going to be a *thing* for the long haul. But, at this particular moment, she was at least seven shots deep, and, hey, the past was the past. Right? Her favorite song started pumping through the speakers. She grabbed Felix's hand.

"Come on, loser. Let's dance."

Felix laughed, "OK, Jane. But only because I want to... Not because you intimidate the hell out of me or anything!"

Jane, Felix, and their friends had a spectacular, fun-filled night. When they finally shut the place down and hailed their respective rides home, Felix, somehow, ended up in the back seat of Jane's Uber.

CHAPTER 15

The Fortune Magazine Interview

Jane stepped into *Fortune Magazine's* office in San Francisco and was greeted in the lobby by a brunette woman.

"Hello! You must be Jane. I'm Erika Fry."

"Great to meet you, Erika."

"The pleasure is all mine. I am so excited to finally have the opportunity to tell your story! You have created quite the buzz in the past year."

Erika Fry's resume was almost as awesome as Jane's. She was a graduate of Dartmouth and Columbia, and she had been writing for *Fortune* for fifteen years. During that time, she had authored some of the publication's most admired stories.

After a quick tour of the office they settled into a small conference room and kicked-off the interview. "So, Jane, you made your first fortune with a mechanical engineering invention. You designed a robot that autonomously builds algae tubes in the desert. You totally revolutionized that industry, but your real expertise is genetic engineering, correct?"

"Yes, I'm a dual-major. My family tree is infested with geneticists and engineers, so combining those two passions seemed to make sense. My parents always encouraged me to build things with my hands, even when I was little. When my dad was in college, he and my grandpa built a human powered flying machine. They flew it at Red Bull's *Flugtag* in Long Beach in front of 100,000 people.

"You mean that crazy event where people ride flying pigs, push them off a 30-foot-tall platform and crash them into the ocean?"

"That's the one. But my father's machine actually flew, at least for a little while."

"So, invention is in your blood?"

"Or maybe in my DNA. It was probably a healthy mix of genetics, and how I was raised. Nature and nurture, as they say. Whatever it was, it drove an almost unhealthy thirst for knowledge. The more I learn, the more I realize how little I know."

"Speaking of your upbringing, your Dad is Adam Stewart -- formerly the Assistant Director at the NSA, but he's now serving in the White House as the Assistant Chief of Staff to President Fernstrom? Tell us a little bit more about him."

"My dad is incredible. His new job definitely keeps him busy. He's essentially on the clock 24-7. We, literally, see more of him on TV standing behind the President, than we see him in person. My mom wishes that he would retire, but he considers it an honor to serve his country. It's not easy. We miss him, but we are very proud of him."

"Obviously, this issue of our magazine is about self-made millionaires under thirty, but you are fairly unique in that you made your first million when you were only twenty."

"Technically, yes. I got the bonus check, and stock options, when I was twenty. But I did most of the work when I was nineteen."

"It looks like you have now redirected your focus almost exclusively to the field of genetics? Do you miss getting your hands dirty with *real* engineering work?"

"I have no problem finding ways to get my hands dirty. But, yes, most of the research that I now do revolves around genetics. I seem to have a knack for it, and the CRISPR tools just keep getting better every year. The opportunities in that field are just incredible. It seems silly to not make genetics my primary focus."

"I've heard rumors that genomic companies pay you as much as $90,000 per week to do research for them, or just to review their research. Is that true?"

"I don't discuss exact numbers when it comes to my personal finances, but, yes, I'm doing OK financially."

"You've made more money at twenty-two years of age than 99% of all humans on the planet will make in their entire lifetimes. Do you ever consider just kicking back retiring?"

"I guess that I could, but I have no plans to retire as long as I love what I am doing. Being able to pick and choose exactly what sort of research I do; that luxury makes the work I end up doing truly enjoyable. I feel very fortunate."

When *Fortune Magazine's* 2026 edition of *30 under 30* was released, Jane's picture was on the front cover, just as Felix had predicted. It was *Fortune's* best-selling issue in over a decade. This resulted in Jane getting a slew of other interview requests, including television and radio appearances. In no time, genetic-nerd Jane had become a pseudo-celebrity, not only in the U.S., but all over the world.

CHAPTER 16

Those Crazy Athletes

May 20, 2026

Jane's recent fame opened doors to a plethora of new opportunities. Major corporations and Ivy League universities were now actively competing to entice her to perform research at their respective institutions. After some deliberation, Jane decided that her next stop would be the University of Pennsylvania's school of medicine, doing genomic research with Dr. Lee Sweeney, a senior professor of physiology and medicine. Jane had long admired Dr. Sweeney's work, having met him at a conference the previous year, and Dr. Sweeney had been equally impressed with Jane.

Sweeney had published dozens of research papers throughout his distinguished career. Those papers were usually presented at technical conferences, or published in obscure scientific journals, with little or no feedback. Dr. Sweeney was accustomed to receiving maybe a few emails or phone calls from his peers about any one paper. But the reaction to the paper that he had recently published with Jane was a completely different animal.

Jane walked into Dr. Sweeney's office as he was staring in disbelief at his computer screen.

"More emails?" asked Jane.

Dr. Sweeney looked up and sighed, "Yes. From high school kids, college football players, crazy-ass parents, coaches, you name it! Ever since *USA Today* published that overly-simplified summary of our paper, the emails have been non-stop."

The paper that was creating all this commotion was focused on Sweeney and Jane's use of CRISPR-created gene therapy to create super-muscular mice.

"These insane people want to use our mouse therapies on humans. And they want to do it immediately. Not for any tangible medical reason. Not because their kids have muscular dystrophy or some other horrible disease. These parents and coaches want to use genetic engineering to make their mediocre high school athletes, slightly less mediocre," Dr. Sweeney fumed.

Jane shook her head, "Don't they understand the risks?"

"They may not comprehend the *full* scope of the risks, but, yes, the scary part is that these crazy-ass parents seem to understand many of the risks. And they are still perfectly willing to volunteer their kids as guinea pigs."

Jane pointed to the screen and laughed, "This kid wants to inject his entire high school football team, and is asking to have it delivered before their conference playoffs."

Dr. Sweeney and Jane's discovery involved injecting a CRISPR-modified gene into mice that tricked their bodies into creating an abundance of a hormone called "insulin-like growth factor". After two months, the treated mice were, on average, 30% stronger and had one third more muscle than the untreated mice.

"I just wish that everyone would understand that there should be decades of research and testing before we even consider testing this gene therapy on humans."

"I don't think that they understand much of anything."

Jane frowned, "I'm worried that the toothpaste is already out of tube. I've heard rumors that thoroughbred horse breeders are already using CRISPR-created gene-doping to do something like our mouse experiment, but that they are using it to make their horses run faster."

"Yes. They *claim* that they are only doing it to help their horses recover faster from injuries, *not* to enhance their performance." Sweeney responded.

"Sure," replied Jane. "That's the same excuse that Lance Armstrong, Barry Bonds and every other performance-enhancing drug-abuser has used for decades."

Dr. Sweeney nodded. "Those drugs *do* support recovery by helping torn muscles heal faster, but that is *not* usually the reason that they're being used."

Jane sighed. "Every time I hear about people wanting to rush these things to market I think of poor Jesse Gelsinger."

Dr. Sweeney hesitated. "But, in *that* case, we were *extremely* cautious. It's not like we were merely trying to improve some football player's forty-yard dash time. We were using gene therapy – the best that we had at the time -- to help a kid fight a crippling disease. We were trying to change his life."

Jesse Gelsinger had suffered from a genetically inherited liver disease his entire life. The disease wasn't immediately terminal, it was somewhat manageable with drugs and a strict diet. But, regardless, it was still a serious hindrance to his life. When Jessie was eighteen, he volunteered to undergo an experimental genetic treatment developed at the University of Pennsylvania. The treatment was designed to be a root-cause cure for Jesse's disease at the genetic level. Unfortunately, things did not go well at all. And, to this day, no one fully understands exactly why.

One complication was that the scientists couldn't merely inject new or modified DNA molecules into Jesse's body and expect them to "take". The researchers had to create a "vehicle", a specifically selected virus, to deliver the DNA precisely to the correct cells in his body. When most of us think of viruses we think of those that cause disease, but the truth is that most viruses are not harmful. Most viruses are either helpful or neutral. The scientists at the University of Pennsylvania had selected a neutral virus to deliver the DNA to cure Jesse's genetic liver disease, so there shouldn't have been any negative reaction. Unfortunately, almost immediately after the treatment, Jesse's body temperature shot up to dangerous levels. A crack-team of elite doctors tried desperately to save him, but nothing worked. One by one, Jessie's organs began to shut down. A few days later his dad made the agonizing decision to have Jesse removed from life support, and he passed away.

Around the same time there were two so-called "bubble boys" in France. They each suffered from a genetic defect which left them with essentially no immune system. Both volunteered to undergo gene therapy to correct their genetic defects and rebuild their non-existent immune systems. The therapy worked extremely well in terms of curing their disease. Both patients regained their immune systems, but this story also lacked a happy ending. Tragically, both boys later developed leukemia and died. The exact genetic link between the therapy and the leukemia still isn't clear, but the likelihood of both boys contacting leukemia at the same time, merely by chance, is so slim that the gene therapy was assumed to have been the cause.

Jane rubbed her temples, "There are far more unknowns here than we could ever imagine. How is this ever going to be controlled or regulated? You and I certainly aren't going to give these kids muscle-building gene mutation therapy. But eventually some lab in the Chinese hinterlands with a CRISPR kit and a website doing untraceable transactions in Bitcoin will gladly sell these kids whatever they want."

Jane had solved many difficult problems in her short life, but she had no idea how this puzzle would turn out in the end.

CHAPTER 17

The Height Gene

June 19, 2026

Jane and Cindy met at a local park for their morning run at 6 am on a beautiful spring morning.

"Ready to get your butt kicked, Jane?"

"Your idle trash talk does not phase me, Grasshopper! But, I *have* been feeling kind of crappy lately. I don't know if it's a stomach bug or what, but it's been kicking my ass."

"I don't want to hear your lame excuses. You'd better bring it."

"OK, fine! Let's hit the bricks."

The friends trekked down the sidewalk as the sun started peeking through the trees.

"So, how'd your date with that ASU basketball player go on Friday?" Jane asked.

"Eh, pretty good. He's a little boring, but he's tall. So, he's got that going for him."

"Isn't he like 6'6?"

"6'8." Cindy corrected.

"That's insane!" Jane exclaimed.

"What can I say? I like a man with height," Cindy shrugged her shoulders. "So, you're the gene freak. Is there something wrong with him? Could the fact that a guy is freakishly tall be an indicator of some other genetic problem that I should be aware of?"

Jane laughed, "Well, genes *are* responsible for around 80% of a person's height, or lack there-of. There are at least 1,000 small variations in our genomes that relate to the composition of connective tissues and bones, and those are the big drivers when it comes to height. But any single genetic variation will only add or subtract around one or two millimeters to the length of any given bone. For someone to be seven feet tall, that might require several *hundred* of these one-millimeter genetic mutations. But factors like diet can also contribute to a person's ultimate height, as well as occasional maladies such as pituitary gland issues."

"So, you're saying that being freakishly tall is *not* any sort of a red flag?"

"As long as he doesn't have some sort of hormonal imbalance, or a pituitary tumor, which is causing him to continuously grow at an alarming rate, then no, he should be totally normal. Although, he may have a serious mental defect if he wants to date you." Jane joked.

"That was un-called for!" Cindy yelled, as she picked up the pace.

At the four-mile mark Jane began to slow a bit. Cindy slowed with her. She glanced several times at the now lethargic pace displayed on her GPS-enabled Garmin watch, but she didn't say anything.

As they rounded a turn near the five-mile mark, Jane yelled. "Hold up a second!"

Jane hobbled to an Oleander bush and vomited. Cindy sprinted over and pulled her friend's hair back as she dry-heaved for another two minutes.

"I think that we'd better head back," said Jane as she slowly stood upright.

"Oh, you think?" Cindy handed Jane her water bottle then took out her phone. "I'm calling an Uber."

Jane shook her head, "No. This has happened before, I get sick, then I bounce back. I can still make it home."

"No way, Jane. We are going to Uber home, get you cleaned up, and then I'm taking you straight to Urgent Care."

Jane had a feeling that she knew what the doctor at Urgent Care was going to say. He came back into the room, and he confirmed it by announcing, "Congratulations, Jane! You're pregnant."

"Pregnant?" Cindy exclaimed, "but, how? Who?"

Jane sat in silence on the examination table with her head in her hands.

"Oh, my god...Felix?" Cindy asked.

Jane lifted her head and let out a long sigh, "Felix."

CHAPTER 18

The Intelligence Genes

June 29, 2026

Jane was dead tired as her black cab weaved through the foggy streets of downtown London. She hadn't been able to sleep on the plane. Flying through seven time zones had turned her morning sickness into all-day sickness. And the gloomy weather wasn't helping her struggle to stay awake either. At least she hadn't rented a car this time. She tried that the last time she visited the UK. Between all the roundabouts, and having to drive on the left side of the road instead of the right, the whole process had made her a nervous wreck.

Coming from Heathrow, her _Hackney Carriage_, as the English refer to their taxi cabs, passed by Kensington Palace and Royal Albert Hall before pulling into Imperial College to pick up Dr. Michael Johnson.

"Good morning, Dr. Johnson!" Jane said as she slid over in the rear seat of the cab to make room, "It's so great to finally meet you."

"The pleasure is all mine Miss Stewart. You have created quite a splash in the...Wow!... You are really young!" Dr. Johnson exclaimed finally looking over at Jane as he fastened his seatbelt. He then shook his head, remembering his manners, "I am so sorry. I didn't mean anything negative by that. I guess I'm used to being surrounded by old geezers like myself in this field."

"Please. Don't give it a second thought, Dr. Johnson," Jane laughed. "I hear that all the time. But I must admit, right now, with this jet-lag hitting me, I feel several decades older than my actual age."

"King's College is very close," replied Dr. Johnson pointing in a northeasterly direction. "We'll be there in no time. And I promise to keep this initial meeting as short as possible."

The black cab passed London's iconic Harrods ultra-high-end department store. It circled the Wellington gate, and then down Constitution Hill. They passed Buckingham Palace on the right, and then weaved over to Victoria Street passing Westminster Abby, Big Ben and Parliament. They cruised down the North shore of the River Thames, zipping past Cleopatra's needle. Shortly after passing under the Waterloo Bridge, the cabbie made a hard left turn onto *The Strand*, entering the historic main campus of King's College London. After a left on Fetter Lane, they rolled to a stop at the front door of King's famous Maughan Library.

As Jane and Dr. Johnson exited the cab they were greeted by Dr. Ian Smith, the Dean of King's College London's School of Genetics.

"Miss Stewart! Dr. Johnson! Such an honor to have the two of you here as our guests at KCL." Dr. Smith shook both their hands with enthusiasm. "Please follow me."

The cool damp air temporarily zapped Jane out of her daze. She was enamored with all the history surrounding her as they strolled through the grounds.

"King's was founded in the early eighteen-hundreds, right? By King George IV?" Jane asked.

Dr. Smith chimed in, "Yes. We pride ourselves in being one of the world's most prestigious research universities. We have minted over a dozen Nobel laureates."

"I'd *kill* for a Nobel Peace Prize" Jane mused.

"To my knowledge none of our alumnae had to go to such measures to get one," Dr. Smith chuckled. "But we have contributed to the discovery of the structure of DNA, and the Higgs boson -- the so-called 'god particle'. We also pioneered in-vitro fertilization and cloning. And, before that, we were instrumental in the invention of radar, television, and several key elements that enable cell phone technology."

"You're really just a bunch of slackers, aren't you?" Dr. Johnson joked.

The DNA comment jogged Jane's memory, "Rosalind Franklin worked here, didn't she? This is where she created that famous *Photo 51*, the x-ray crystallography image that led Watson and Crick to discover the double helix structure of DNA?"

"Yes, she did. Unfortunately, Rosalind was only 37 when she died from cancer. During her short lifetime, she didn't get nearly the credit she deserved. But, over time, her slight has been somewhat rectified. There's a play showing right here in London's West End about Rosalind Franklin's life. Nicole Kidman plays the role of Rosalind, whenever she's in town. I can have my assistant get some tickets for you."

"Really? That would be incredible! Thank you, Dr. Johnson." Jane beamed with excitement, "And honestly, how cool is it that an A-list celebrity like Nicole Kidman is playing a genetic research scientist?"

"Maybe there's hope yet for us researchers to finally be considered 'cool'!" quipped Dr. Johnson.

"I wouldn't go that far." responded Jane. "I was on the cover of *Fortune* magazine and I still manage to bore my friends to death at happy hour whenever I talk about what I do for a living. They still think that I'm the most un-cool person they know!"

Jane's upbeat mood was suddenly sobered when she recalled that it would be at least seven months before she could partake in another happy hour with her friends. Earlier that week she had called Felix to tell him that she was pregnant. He immediately grew defensive and claimed that it couldn't possibly be his kid, since they used protection. Even after Jane explained to him that no precautions could be 100% effective, Felix accused her of lying. He claimed that she was only saying the baby was his to could "trap and control" him again. The call ended with Jane hanging up in anger, and they hadn't spoken since.

Dr. Smith, Dr. Johnson and Jane entered the Maughan Library's historic Round Reading Room for their meeting.

The gray London sky could be seen through the massive glass dome above the large table in the middle of the rotunda.

Jane looked around the room and smiled, "It's a dodecagon!"

Dr. Smith laughed, "Good eye! Yes, the dome is actually twelve-sided, not round, but '*The Dodecagonal Reading Room*' doesn't exactly roll off the tongue, now does it?"

"Wasn't this room mentioned in Dan Brown's novel *The Da Vinci Code*?" Jane asked.

"Yes, but the room didn't make it into the movie."

"Yet another example of your prestigious institution slacking, Ian!" jeered Dr. Johnson while patting Dr. Smith on the back. The trio sat down at the table and the meeting commenced.

"In the interest of saving time, I am going to cut to the quick regarding why I wanted us to meet," stated Dr. Johnson. "For millennium, people have believed that at least some portion of a person's intelligence was inherited. This is the theory that has been used to perpetuate the whole concept of royal, genetic, class-based systems, all base on heredity. The theory was that only those with royal pedigree, good blood-lines, had the genetic superiority, the inherited intellect, and the required leadership skills to run an empire."

Dr. Smith chimed in, "That was back when the royal families had *real* authority. When the news of the day was about whose heads the royals were cutting off – not just gossip about who the prince might be dating that week."

"Exactly." Dr. Johnson continued. "And then, during the so-called '*Enlightenment*' that entire royal genetic superiority concept was totally rejected and dismissed.

Royal aristocratic governments were dumped in favor of democracies. But now, things seem to have come full-circle. Current genetic studies overwhelmingly indicate that up to 75% of IQ is genetic, while only 25% is driven by things like schooling, family, friends and other forcing functions."

"Yes. We had similar results here at King's College," Dr. Smith added. "By comparing GCSE's -- similar to American high school grade point averages – our studies found that around 65% of those grade differences were due to genetics."

"But how did you determine that those differences were genetic?" Jane asked. "How could you rule out all of the other possible causes?"

"In our case, we studied twins. 12,000 of them. 6,000 pairs. 3,000 pairs of maternal twins and 3,000 pairs of fraternal twins. The GCSE results were highly heritable. It was clear that genes explained a huge proportion of the academic differences between children."

"Interesting," Jane paused then continued her questioning. "The previous consensus was that intelligence was mostly determined by the formation of the cerebral cortex, right? The grey matter, the outermost layer of the human brain?"

"Yes," answered Dr. Smith. "And we still agree that grey matter plays a key role in memory, attention, perceptual awareness, thought, and language. Coincidentally, our research shows that grey matter levels are genetically driven as well."

"One problem, of course, is that these studies and statistics are rarely published." Dr. Johnson added.

"That's because they suggest the exact opposite of everything that our modern society is based on. It flies in the face of the concept that 'all men are created equal'. No one wants to publicly support any inference that a person's intellect -- or lack there-of -- is primarily determined at birth, based on their blood-line." Dr. Smith stated.

"It is definitely a touchy subject, but I think it's fair to say that everyone in this room is on the same page, that genetics plays a huge role in intelligence. Our big question is, which genes are relevant? Which ones are the key drivers of IQ?" Dr. Johnson smiled, "I'm here today to tell you that my colleagues and I at London Imperial College have concluded that two specific networks of genes appear to determine whether people are intelligent or, shall we say, not so intelligent. We found that the same genes that influence human intelligence in healthy people were also the genes that cause impaired cognitive ability when mutated. We refer to these genetic networks as M1 and M3."

Jane eyes grew wide, "Are you saying that you may have found a genetic 'master switch' for intelligence?"

"Sort of. There are over a thousand IQ alleles which account for the actual IQ variation that we see in the general population." Dr. Smith added.

Jane nodded in agreement and began speaking quickly, thinking out loud. "Which means that 100 or so *additional* positive gene variants could raise a person's IQ by fifteen points?"

Her head was spinning as the data started to make sense, "And 200 positive gene variants could raise IQ by thirty points? That's huge!"

"Yes," Dr. Johnson exclaimed, still smiling, "and if a human could be engineered to have the positive version of *every* causal IQ-gene variant, they might exhibit cognitive ability which is roughly 100 standard deviations above average. That would correspond to an IQ of more than 1,000 points!"

Jane rocked back in her chair. "What could a nation accomplish if it increased every citizen's IQ by thirty or forty points? What if a country could turn all of its citizens into geniuses?

"Or, taken to the extreme, what could a person accomplish with an IQ of 1,000?" Dr. Johnson started thinking out loud, "Could you imagine? What would that be like?"

A man named William James Sidis probably had the highest IQ of any human in history. His IQ was somewhere between 250 and 300, several times higher than the average human IQ of 100. William was accepted at Harvard when he was eleven years of age and he earned a degree in mathematics. After graduation, Harvard employed him as a math professor while he was still a young teenager. William, however, was socially awkward and he had few, if any, friends. He also ran into several legal problems. Eventually, William found himself in a mental institution, placed there by his parents to 'cure' him of his infatuation with socialist and communist political movements. In the end, William turned his back on all scholarly endeavors, and died at forty-six years of age from a brain hemorrhage.

Other individuals with ultra-high-IQs have fared much better. Terence Tao's IQ is around 225. Terence won a *Fields Medal* back in 2006 and still works as a professor at UCLA where he researches harmonic analysis and other fields of mathematics.

Garry Kasparov the world's number-one grand-master chess player for nearly twenty years, had an IQ of around 194.

IQ tests didn't exist when Leonardo da Vinci was alive, but his IQ is estimated to have been around 185. Leonardo, of course, was extremely successful in many fields including engineering, sculpting, music, mathematics, astronomy, and painting.

Albert Einstein never took an IQ test, but experts estimate his IQ to have been in the 160 to 190 range.

And there sat Dr. Johnson, daydreaming about the potential of a human with a ludicrous IQ of 1,000.

Jane shook her head, "We're playing with fire here, gentlemen."

Dr. Johnson smiled. "Fire can heat your house and cook your food!"

"Fire can also burn down entire cities," Jane frowned. "Let's roll the marble and game this thing out. If a complete, predictive genetic IQ model were available, it could be used in a variety of reproductive applications, right? It could be used for embryo selection."

"Sure," stated Dr. Johnson, "We could create some sort of a predictive genetic IQ score to choose which IVF zygotes to implant. By choosing only embryos with the highest IQ-potential, parents could improve the average IQ of their children by at least fifteen points."

"That's the difference between a kid who's only an average high school student, versus a Magna Cum Laude college graduate." Dr. Smith chimed in.

"On the other hand, an alternative to passive selection would be active genetic editing. With CRISPR, we could alter as many IQ genes as we wished. The IQ improvements for any infant could be virtually unlimited." Jane's head started to spin, thinking of the possibilities.

"People are going to jump all over this," Dr. Smith added. "Even if these genetic IQ treatments cost five or ten thousand dollars, that's still far less than the tuition at a high-end private pre-school. And, it is a proven fact that even the most expensive, elite private pre-schools make little or no difference in terms of long-term IQ scores and ultimate outcomes."

"But how will this happen?" asked Jane, "Who will decide which babies get these genetic IQ improvements and how big those genetic IQ improvements will be? Will it be the parents? The government? Will there be limits?"

Dr. Johnson shrugged, "Each country will decide for itself where to draw the line. Labs in some countries are already providing genetic engineering for profit, catering exclusively to the world's rich and famous. Parents who are willing to pay top dollar to have little Einstein-babies created for them."

Jane nodded, "Yes, but, as with other technologies, only the early adopters will have to pay through the nose. Eventually, I believe that countries will not only legalize human genetic engineering, they may even make it an optional part of their free national healthcare systems."

Dr. Johnson shook his head, "I disagree with the *optional* part. I think that countries will eventually *require* IQ genetic engineering, as they now require vaccinations for tuberculosis and polio. It will eventually evolve to the point that parents who refuse to have their children genetically engineered will be arrested and charged with child abuse."

Jane scoffed, "Come on, Dr. Johnson. You're getting a bit delusional now."

Dr. Johnson chuckled. "Miss Jane. You are not the first person to call me delusional, but this time, I beg to differ. I am *positive* that I will be proven right."

"But it's so risky to be testing these things on humans," Jane argued. "Maybe we can try it on chimps first. Is a chimp's IQ determined by genetics too? Or is it more a function of training by humans?"

"No. We found that training has almost no effect on a chimp's IQ. Their IQ is almost entirely controlled by genetics. Chimpanzees raised by humans turn out to be no smarter than those raised in the wild."

"Or, maybe it only proves that humans are no better parents than chimps." Dr. Smith quipped.

Dr. Johnson nodded, "That is definitely a possibility. Our study involved 100 chimps, ages nine to fifty-two. The tests involved cognitive tasks testing a variety of abilities. Training didn't help significantly, nor did environment. Even love and nurturing seemed to have no effect. Genetics trumped all other factors when it came to chimp intelligence."

Jane grimaced, "As a geneticist, I guess that I should find that exciting, but for some reason, it just makes be incredibly sad."

CHAPTER 19

Artificial Intelligence -- The Apocalypse That Wasn't

July 25, 2026

In her spare time, Jane had taken a few million dollars that she found under her couch cushions and started her own small genetic engineering company. She had named it *Geno Design LTD*. Early one morning Jane was sipping her coffee as she listened to the soothing hum of hundreds of spinning disk drives and power supply fans servicing the bank of hundreds of nVIDIA neural network computers. Jane had personally programed those computers to iteratively create the precise DNA CRISPR edits required to fix whatever human ailment she happened to be focusing on that day. Her best friend, and now VP of marketing, Cindy Murray sauntered into the lab.

"Hey Jane. I've got a new geek joke for you."

"Okay," Jane replied as she looked up from her computer monitors, "Let's hear it."

"What does a biologist wear on a date?"

"I haven't the slightest clue."

"Designer genes! Get it? Like denim jeans, but instead it's spelt like a genetic gene? Not only is this joke witty, but it also ties into our company's name, and the overall brand." Cindy dramatically tapped her head with her index finger, "Creative marketing at its finest. This is why us marketing majors make the big bucks."

Jane shook her head, "Don't quit your day job, babe."

"Might I remind you that this *is* my day job. The one that you pay me to do, so you better think it's funny too or we're both in trouble."

"Fine, it's funny. You're the best. I don't know what I'd do without you." Jane responded sarcastically.

Cindy smiled, "That's what I like to hear, boss."

Jane's eyes went back to her computer screen as she started typing again, tweaking and optimizing her genetic neural network software. Meanwhile, Cindy's eyes scanned around the room, taking note of the seemingly endless banks of GPU computers and servers that were cluttering Jane's lab.

"You know, Jane... years ago, I remember a bunch of really smart people like Gates, Musk, and Hawking, *all* predicting that, by now, Artificial Intelligence would be the master of the universe. That A.I. was going to wipe out mankind. Just like that asteroid annihilated the dinosaurs. Those guys would be pretty impressed if they saw you here today, with these evil computers under your tyrannical human thumb."

"I never bought into that 'all powerful A.I.' crap," replied Jane, not looking up from her work. "Maybe a thousand years from now, but certainly not in our lifetimes. The theory was that the never-ending march of Moore's Law would eventually enable human-level intelligence in machines. Fortunately for us, replacing people with A.I. isn't nearly as easy as everyone first thought. At least not for most tasks."

Moore's Law (named after the founder of *Intel*) states that computer memory and throughput will double every eighteen months. Ever since Gordy Moore stated his *'law'*, back in 1965, it has proven to be surprisingly accurate. As chip feature sizes shrank to near the wavelength of visible light, many believed that Moore's law would break down, but engineers found clever ways to make the masks *quantum physics friendly* – and just like that, Moore's Law kept marching on.

Jane continued babbling while simultaneously manipulating the information on six banks of computer screens like *Emerson, Lake and Palmer* performing a concert. "The Artificial Intelligence apocalypse prophets believed that the march of Moore's Law would eventually result in computers that were massively superior to the human brain. They theorized that computers would achieve human-like consciousness and would begin thinking on their own."

"Haven't they already done that?" Cindy asked. "Computers have beaten the smartest humans at *Jeopardy*, and they've beaten Grand Masters in chess tournaments. They did that years ago."

"Sure. Computers do well in those examples, but they aren't really *thinking*. They just blindly attempt millions of potential moves in fractions of a second. Then they use whichever move happens to yield the best result. They aren't thinking, they're just guessing really fast. Machines will never become self-aware in my lifetime."

"I don't know. It still scares me."

Jane looked up from her computer at her stubborn-minded friend. She leaned back in her chair and continued refining her point. "Think about it this way – Let's say that you have a mega-server-farm, inside a huge 40,000 square-foot climate-controlled building. In that case, you would have *almost* enough memory and computational muscle to approach the capabilities of a human brain, somewhere in the neighborhood two billion mega-flops of processing power and three quadrillion bytes of memory. But, that server-farm requires a dedicated natural-gas-fired power-plant to create the megawatts required to power not only the servers, but also to run all of the chillers which are needed to ensure that those high-powered servers don't melt."

"What's your point?"

"The human brain only consumes around 20 watts. A brain is approximately two hundred thousand times more efficient, less power hungry, than an 'equivalent' man-made server farm. And, efficiency is very important if you're a robot with a hankering to partake in world domination."

"Fair point." Cindy conceded, but Jane wasn't done quite yet.

"In addition to memory and throughput, the third key performance parameter is input and output, or I/O, capability. A human brain simultaneously processes inputs from millions of nerve sensors. It also outputs precise analog electrical signals to control thousands of individual groups of muscle fibers. There has never been a computer in history that has controlled as many individual I/O circuits as the human brain does every hour of every day. That's because the human brain is massively parallel, whereas computers are primarily serial devices."

Cindy interrupted, "That's not true. My laptop is parallel. I can be on six different web sites, while running Word, Excel, Power Point, and a dozen other apps, all at the same time."

"It may *seem* like your computer is doing all those things in parallel, but it isn't. Each processor core is only doing one simplistic operation at a time. But a human brain can truly do millions of tasks concurrently. And the human brain accesses general ideas, while computers operate by accessing data located at a specific memory address. That's why computers and robots can't perform most of the simplest human tasks, and probably never will."

"I guess it's hard for me to believe that, because looking around here, it sure seems like you're relying on your computer minions to do your genetic engineering work for you." Cindy stated emphatically while staring at Jane's massive array of machines.

"Yes. They are great at *this* job. I couldn't do it without them; but when it comes to rudimentary tasks like sorting and folding a pile of laundry, computers suck. Almost 200,000 lines of code were required to train one robot to fold one specific type of towel. And, the robot was still laughably slow at folding that towel. The YouTube video is hilarious. To be 'equal' to humans, a robot shouldn't have to be programmed to fold laundry. It should be able to learn how to fold laundry merely by watching a human fold laundry for an hour or so, just like humans are trained when they get a job in a hotel's laundry room for minimum wage."

Cindy slowly nodded her head. "I guess that makes sense, but then why were those smart billionaires all so worried -- raging against the machines so-to-speak -- if AI-enabled robots are really so damn stupid that they can't even fold a beach towel?"

"Don't say that too loud. The servers are listening!" Jane cupped her hand over her mouth to prevent the servers from hearing her. The friends broke into laughter.

"I think that those old-school-billionaires were looking at the big picture without fully understanding everything required to make robots truly worthy matches to us human beings. It's more than just matching the human brain's memory and throughput. AI-computers aren't going to take over the world any time soon, but for tasks like genetic editing, they are ideal. Before I started using artificial intelligence, I could only find the 'obvious' edits to achieve relatively simplistic genetic results. But, with the help of neural-net super-computers, I can create almost anything."

"So, people should stop worrying about AI-robots and we should *really* be worried about genetic-geniuses like you, Ms. Frankenstein?" Cindy joked.

Jane laughed, but deep down, she knew that Cindy was probably right.

CHAPTER 20

A Promotion to Service

President Michael Fernstrom paced back and forth in front of his desk in the oval office. He was thinking out loud as a throng of White House staffers stood along the back wall taking notes. Above their heads, five flat-screen TV's were streaming a non-stop barrage of investigations and sexual harassment charges against various members of President Fernstrom's administration. As if he didn't already have enough problems on his plate, he now had to tackle the media's criticism regarding his administration's lack of diversity, which the press referred to as "a fraternity of old white guys."

"Any ideas, people?" Fernstrom asked his staff as he scanned the room. "Anything?"

His entire staff kept their heads down and scribbled in their note pads, trying avoid making eye-contact with their boss. Not a single new idea was offered. The silence was deafening.

"Holy shit, people. What are the American people paying you for?" Fernstrom walked briskly back to his desk. He noticed a dog-eared *Fortune* magazine lying in a pile of publications on the corner of the Oval Office's legendary *Theodore Roosevelt Desk*. The President grabbed the publication, stared at the cover for a moment, and then lifted his head.

"Adam Stewart!" The president looked around the room. "Where the hell is Adam?"

Chip Willing answered, "Adam is outside in the hall, sir. But I can answer any questions that you have."

Adam Stewart, Jane's father, was President Fernstrom's Deputy Chief of Staff. But, on the org chart, he officially reported to the President's Chief of Staff, Chip Willing. Adam had recently made the mistake of performing a bit too well and getting himself into the President's good graces. In retaliation, Chip, had asked Adam to remain outside the Oval Office during the President's daily staff meetings.

"No, Chip," replied the President. "Obviously, you can't answer my questions because, 30 seconds ago, I asked for your ideas and you provided as much creative input as a damn rutabaga. So kindly get your worthless ass into that damn hallway and get Adam back in here, now!"

The Chief of Staff scampered into the hallway while kicking himself for not keeping his resume and LinkedIn career profiles up-to-date.

Fernstrom stood behind his desk and addressed the remaining staff members who were now petrified with fear. "Now open your damn ears and listen to me for once! We just lost our Secretary of Health and Human Services to a charge of sexual misconduct with an intern. Now I honestly do not care how you all get your rocks off, but holy crap, make sure that whomever you are doing is over 18, preferably over 21, get their consent, and keep your grimy hands off the damn interns! Do you understand?"

The terrified group of senior staff-members murmured various confirmations of understanding to their leader.

"Good. Now that we are all on the same page with that issue, what replacement nominees do we have ready to go for HHS Secretary?"

"Well, we're still in the very early stages of vetting candidates, Mr. President. It could take a while... We want to make sure..."

"My ass it will take a while!" screamed Fernstrom as Adam Stewart entered the room with no idea of why he was being pulled-in. The president grabbed the copy of *Fortune* magazine from his desk and waved it in the air.

"Adam! This your daughter on the cover, right?"

Mere seconds earlier, Adam had been sitting on the floor in a West Wing hallway, marking-up legislation on his laptop. Now he was standing in the Oval Office with the commander-in-chief waving a picture of his daughter in his face.

"Yes, sir. That's my daughter, Jane, Mr. President."

Fernstrom turned his attention back towards the rest of his staff, "Gentlemen, have you read this article?" Again, the response was total silence – nothing but deer-in-the-headlights stares. "Well I *have* read it. Adam's kid is smarter, and has accomplished more in her 22 years, than all of you in this room have accomplished, combined, in all your years on this planet. Why the hell isn't she our candidate for HHS Secretary? How many of your present candidates are women? How many of them can do genetic engineering in their sleep? How many are under the age of 40?"

After an uncomfortably long silence, Chip finally spoke up. "So far, sir, they are all men. And I believe that they are all over 50. Actually, they may all be over 60."

The president was now fuming. "Are you all completely tone-deaf! Don't you listen to what the talking heads are saying?" He pointed to the TVs mounted on the wall.

"Here is what is going to happen. You are going to spend the next three days vetting the crap out of Adam's daughter, uh…" The president had to look at the magazine cover again because he had already forgotten her name.

Adam chimed in, "Jane, sir."

"Yes, of course, Jane. You are going to vet Jane, and then we are going to get her ass approved by the Senate in record time. Because it would be political suicide for any of those old bastards in the Senate to vote against a young, bright, accomplished, and untainted woman."

The president turned to Adam, "Your daughter would accept the nomination, right? It pays around $290,000 per year."

Adam was somewhat at a loss for words. "Mr. President, my daughter is her own person, I certainly don't speak for her. I know that she is booked solid with running her new company, speeches and appearances. But if she wants the position, money won't be a factor. She'll probably donate the salary to charity."

"Done deal," the president smiled and returned to his desk, thrilled that he had accomplished at least this one productive task this miserable day.

"There is one other thing worth mentioning, sir." Adam interjected. "You should know that Jane is nearly four months pregnant, out of wedlock."

"Hmmm. Can we get her to marry the baby-daddy within the next week or so?" asked Fernstrom.

"No, sir. As far as I know he wants nothing to do with her, or the baby."

Fernstrom stroked his chin for a moment as he thought through this particular wrinkle.

"Hell, it's 2026. If anything, the whole *'strong, independent woman who don't need no man'* crap will make her even more favorable in the polls. Vet her!"

In the end, Jane's appointment to be the Secretary of HHS went smoother than even President Fernstrom had anticipated. Democrat and Republican senators were tripping over each other to be supportive of her appointment. The hearings devolved into a Jane-love-fest, as senators swooned over her for their own political gain. Despite President Fernstrom's record-low approval ratings, Jane was confirmed unanimously to become the youngest cabinet member in U.S. history -- beating out the previous holder of that record, Alexander Hamilton, by ten years.

CHAPTER 21

The Old Age Gene

Lee Koenig was sitting in the reception area outside of the U.S. Government's Health and Human Services (HHS) executive offices in Washington D.C. The concrete and glass building was located a few blocks southwest of the nation's Capital building on Independence Avenue. Lee was a VP and senior lobbyist for *Viva Youth Inc.*, the holder of all U.S. patents for the so-called "youth gene".

When Lee was finally ushered into an HHS conference room he was surprised to see not only the new HHS Secretary, Jane Stewart, but also the Director of Medicare, Derek Ernst, whom he already knew, and two other cabinet members whom he did not recognize.

Derek led the introductions. "Thanks for coming, Lee. This is David Herzog, our Assistant Secretary of the Treasury." Lee and David shook hands and exchanged business cards.

"… and this is John Ott, he is our Administrator for the Centers for Medicare & Medicaid Services (CMS). He's a lawyer, but we try not to hold that against him."

"99% of lawyers give the rest of us a bad name," quipped John as he shook Lee's hand and exchanged cards.

Lee quickly handed out his Power Point slides and prepared to give his presentation.

The government officials smiled politely as they set Lee's Power Point decks off to the side. Obviously, Lee was *not* going to be controlling the agenda of this meeting.

John Ott kicked off the discussion. "Thank you so much for coming to see us on such short notice, Mr. Koenig."

"I always appreciate the opportunity to communicate the value of *Viva Youth's* products to our cherished customers," replied Lee, a bit perplexed.

"So, Lee. How is the testing going?" asked David Herzog, getting right to the point.

"Well, as you probably know, the first human tests were performed by our founder Elizabeth Parrish, on herself, almost a decade ago. In the domain of restorative gene therapy, our CEO was essentially 'patient zero'."

"And, as we all know, those experiments went extremely well", added Mr. Ernst.

"Yes," replied Lee. "Her cells were rejuvenated by the genetic therapy. It reversed over twenty years of normal telomere shortening. After her treatment, Ms. Parrish was, genetically, twenty years younger than she had been before the therapy."

The genetic jargon had David Herzog, a finance major, a bit confused. "And, what are these 'telomeres'?" he asked.

Jane, the newly-minted HHS secretary chimed in, "Telomeres are the small portions of DNA that cover and protect the ends of your chromosomes. They are padding. Sort of like a football helmet for chromosomes. Every time that our cells divide, the telomeres get a little shorter. This is the genetic-based cause of what most people refer to as the aging process."

"Exactly," agreed Lee, "Once a person's telomeres are worn down, stem-cell depletion normally occurs next. That depletion is what causes a plethora of age-related infirmities and diseases -- everything from wrinkly skin to organ failure."

Jane pushed the lobbyist for more details. "So, Lee, how exactly do you know that this gene therapy of yours really works? How did you quantify success?"

Lee walked over to the window and looked down the mall at the Washington Monument in the distance. "One way is to use something called a 'Telomere Score'. That score is calculated by measuring the telomere length of chromosomes in a person's white blood cells. We measure the T-lymphocyte telomere length and compare it to an average length for a given age. The result is what we call a person's 'genetic age'".

John Ott shook his head in disbelief. "I still can't believe that your CEO actually went straight from studies on mice, to testing those therapies on herself. Granted, it gave your company a huge lead on everyone else in the industry, but it's still nuts."

"It borders on being unethical." Jane added.

"I respectfully disagree," responded Lee. "First, Liz Parrish tested it on herself, not on a third party. Second, she is a PhD geneticist, so she fully understood all the potential risks. Lastly, and most importantly, she wasn't using this treatment merely to defy father time. She wasn't doing it for vanity. She had some serious ailments. Our initial testing showed that her telomeres were abnormally short considering that she was only forty-four years old at the time. This left her vulnerable to a host of age-related diseases. In her mind, the biggest risk was *not* trying something, even if that *something* was not yet fully tested."

The Assistant Secretary of the Treasury wasn't a huge fan of lobbyists. He scribbled something in his notebook, removed his eye glasses and pointed them accusingly at Lee, "And these results were independently verified? This isn't just a bunch of you bio-tech industry unicorns drinking your own bathwater?"

"Fully peer-reviewed," replied Lee. "Liz's results were independently verified by dozens of labs all over the world. Furthermore, the results have been repeated in many animal, and even a few additional human studies. And now we're using CRISPR tools to *directly* modify DNA. CRISPR has made the therapy even more precise and effective."

Derek Ernst looked over at Jane and grimaced. "Did HHS approve these human studies?"

Lee chuckled, "No, sir, you did not. So far, the FDA, HHS, and all other U.S. Government agencies have refused to approve any of our human studies or tests. All of our human studies, as well as those of our competitors, have been performed off-shore. Which means that other countries are now far ahead of the U.S., not only in terms of this therapy, but in most other areas of human-based genetic research as well."

"And you're sure that we can't achieve these same results with simple lifestyle changes? Exercising? Eating right? Juice cleanses? All that crap?" asked John Ott.

"Smoking can shorten your telomeres. And quitting smoking usually allows those telomeres to grow back a bit. But all the other lifestyle changes that you mentioned seem to have little or no impact on telomere length. Certainly, nothing even close to what we can achieve with biotechnology."

"So, on one hand, this research could be dangerous and unethical," Herzog observed. He was still wary, but as the Assistant Treasury Secretary he couldn't ignore the glimmering dollar signs that he saw in the distance. "On the other hand, if this treatment prevents or cures most age-related diseases, then it could be groundbreaking both medically and financially. Old age maladies are crushing our federal budget, a budget that President Fernstrom has order me to *somehow* keep in balance. All to meet some off-the-cuff campaign-promise that he made three years ago. Our problem here in the U.S. is bad, but it's even worse in counties with exploding elderly populations and insanely low birth rates like Japan, South Korea, Italy, and Greece."

"That is true," Jane replied. "We've been reducing Medicare coverage every year, either by raising deductibles or by limiting care, but our deficits are still soaring. This telomere fix *could* eliminate virtually all of those issues, but I'm not sure...."

"Well I am sure, Jane," interrupted David. He was clearly captivated as he punched some numbers into the calculator app on his phone. "The way I see it, by spending a couple billion dollars right now to genetically modify our senior citizens, we could literally save over three trillion dollars in Medicare expenses over the next decade. That's almost a *thousand-fold* return on investment!"

Shortly after that meeting, in what seemed like the blink of an eye, the U.S. government completely reversed course, primarily due to pressure from the Department of the Treasury. Jane was not nearly as enthusiastic. She fervently opposed fast-tracking the proposal, but she was summarily over-ruled. Instead of prohibiting telomere modification treatments, the federal government began providing lucrative tax credits to *Viva Youth* to help bring their CRISPR-enabled telomere enhancing drugs to the American market even faster.

Mere months later, the U.S. Government was not only offering free telomere treatments to all U.S. citizens, they even began paying $200 cash bonuses to anyone who underwent genetic telomere treatments. By the mid 2030's the Medicare system, which was supposed to go bankrupt, had instead accumulated a surplus of over one trillion dollars. On top of that, U.S. senior citizens were living longer and healthier than ever. David Herzog was primarily credited with concocting the scheme. He was hailed a hero.

CHAPTER 22

The Ethics of Pig Brains

October 18, 2026

Joe Stinebaker was a professor of ethics at Washington University, in University City, Missouri, a few miles outside of St. Louis. He was playing darts with his colleague Mickey O'Halloran, who was a professor of genetic chemistry at Wash-U as well. They were at the Blue Berry Hill tavern on a cool fall evening and Joe was in the middle of one of his legendary tirades.

"Dammit Mickey, how can you not be afraid of these unregulated labs creating chimeras?" asked the ethics professor. "It used to be only a couple dozen labs, but now there are hundreds of chimera labs all over America. Thousands worldwide! Those weasels are using CRISPR to create every sort of mutant animal imaginable."

"Weasels aren't all bad. Eagles may soar, but you never see weasels getting sucked into jet engines," replied Mickey with a hearty laugh. "I do see your point. Some of their creations are a bit Frankenstein-like, but…"

"Frankenstein was fictional," interrupted Joe in a bit of a tizzy. "This is real-life. This isn't about one nut-case in the basement of some gothic castle. Thousands of unregulated mad-scientists are now practicing their dark-arts all over the planet. It's horrifying."

"I couldn't disagree more!" exclaimed the genetics professor as he nailed a bull's eye to end their game. "My niece would be dead right now if it wasn't for the new liver that she got from a CRISPR-created chimera pig. It took her from being near-death to being a beautiful, normal young woman, living life to the fullest. I may not be a certified ethicist like you, but it's going to be a long putt for you to make any ethical arguments that trump my niece's life."

Joe sighed, "But, it's crazy to trust a damn artificial molecule to run around inside a person's body and choose the correct sections of DNA to cut and replace!"

"It's not about trust, it's about science and chemistry. We create a CRISPR key sequence that tells the molecule exactly where to latch onto the DNA molecule, and then exactly where to cut."

"OK. Maybe you can accurately predict which DNA section the CRISPR molecule will cut-out, but how does anyone know exactly which gene will replace it? That fill-process is where all the risk is."

Mickey shook his head. "The DNA fill process is perfectly natural. That's how DNA molecules were designed by God, or by Mother Nature, or by whatever galactic master-force you ethicists believe in today. That's just how the chemistry works. And, it's not unnatural. It's how DNA repairs the natural damage that occurs in your body every day. Those huge DNA molecules are constantly getting damaged by free radicals; age; and even cosmic rays that were generated by distant exploding stars millions of light-years away. If DNA molecules couldn't repair themselves naturally, then life on Earth wouldn't exist."

"Mickey, there is nothing 'natural' about creating mutant chimeras. Those DNA holes aren't accidental, or random -- they're intentional. And, the fill-material is totally unnatural too. Instead of being from the animal itself, it is from a human!"

"I agree that we are steering the natural chemical processes in a few, slightly less than natural directions."

"Do you hear yourself?" Joe scoffed, in complete disbelief. "This is the absolute definition of mad science. Your colleagues are going way too far and moving way too fast. They think that they understand the processes for their *intended* mutation, but they have no understanding of all the *other* possible mutations."

Mickey shook his head in disagreement. "We've heard that tin-foil-hat crap a million times, Joe. Like whether human cells could accidentally create *other* human tissues in the pig…"

"Yes! Exactly! Like the brain!" Joe was on an unstoppable roll, so much so that he hadn't touched his beer in over ten minutes. "What if you are sitting there in your lab creating human pancreases or livers or arm pits or whatever, and occasionally, every thousandth time or so, you create a pig with a human-like brain? What are you going to do then?"

Mickey took a long, deep breath before he answered, "It's not going to happen."

"You don't know that, Mickey! And, worse yet, you probably wouldn't know if it did happen. A pig with a human brain wouldn't have the required vocal cords and oral cavity to speak, but this doesn't change the fact that your mutant pig would have a human's thoughts, soul, and consciousness, right?"

"Yes. That would be ugly," Mickey took a drink of his beer and shrugged. "But it won't happen."

Joe continued, "So, you'd probably just kill the pig, steal its human pancreas and move on. Right? You wouldn't even know that you had just killed a pig with a human consciousness. The only way you'd ever figure it out would be if some medical student happened to notice the odd shape of the pig's brain during a post-mortem dissection in a gross anatomy lab. And, then maybe that over-achieving med-student would to do a DNA test on the pig's brain, just because he was curious to see what was wrong. Only then would he discover that the brain was human. Then what? Do we charge everyone in the lab with first degree murder for killing a human being?"

Mickey sighed, "I don't know, Joe."

"That's why you need to get ethicists involved in the process early-on -- before you find yourself serving thirty-to-life at Sing Sing. That's why Jane Stewart is refusing to fund this type of work. She's the only one left in government with her head screwed on straight."

Mickey laughed, "Stewart's just paranoid and trying to cover her ass. Besides, the lack of HHS funding isn't slowing down my team, or anyone else for that matter. We have more private funding than we can spend. It will all work out in the end, Joe. You just keep dreaming up impossible disaster scenarios, and I'll keep saving human lives."

"Sure," Joe growled at his colleague. "And you'll create even more problems in the process. Like animal viruses getting transferred to humans by those animal-grown transplanted organs. That's another huge area of concern that I have."

"No. We've already fixed that."

"Oh yeah? Do you *know* that you fixed it? Or do you only *think* that you *probably* fixed it?"

"We used CRISPR to inactivate around 80 retrovirus genes in pigs. By doing that, we eliminated the pig-to-human virus-transfer problem. We can now safely use those virus-free pigs to grow human organs," Mickey replied triumphantly.

"Maybe," replied Joe as he threw a bull's eye to even-up their match at one game each. "But now you've created an even more unnatural pig in the process, right? You're just making the problem worse!"

CHAPTER 23

You Can Only
Fight So Long

December 29, 2026

Jane was thirty-eight weeks pregnant and she was beside herself. She was one of the world's foremost genetic engineering experts. As the leader of the U.S. Department of Health and Human Services, she expected her well-informed opinions to be taken seriously, but this no longer seemed to be the case.

"Look Jane, we understand your concerns, but we're getting our clocks cleaned," Derick Ernst pleaded.

David Herzog continued. "And not only by the top-tier G-7 countries. Former third-world countries are going to be beating us like a rug as well."

"Their young citizens are smarter than ours, they are stronger than ours, they have more endurance, and they work harder. This is not only about getting our butts kicked in the Olympics. Our military will become a second or third-rate entity. Our weapons will be fine, but other country's recruits will be wiping the floor with us in terms of physical and mental ability."

"I know, I know," replied Jane, exasperated. She had been fighting this fight ever since her appointment by President Fernstrom, and she was totally worn out.

While most other countries had jumped on-board, and even gone so far as to *require* that their children receive gene-enhancement therapy, Jane had led the effort in the U.S. to do the exact opposite. She had encouraged Congress to prohibit American citizens from even purchasing most types of human gene-enhancement therapy for their children. Encouraging senior citizens to take gene-therapy was one thing. But forcing CRISPR therapies on unwitting children and infants who had no say in the matter, at least in Jane's opinion, was beyond the pale. Jane stared at the ceiling as she felt her baby kicking like Ronda Rousey in a cage match. At this point in her pregnancy, she should have been on maternity leave, but things at the office were so chaotic that she had decided to work right up until the baby arrived.

Jane looked down at her belly and thought of her own child growing up in a world dominated by this science-gone-mad insanity. "No, gentlemen! I'm sorry, I can't condone any of this until we know for sure that it's safe. We need more tests."

"More tests? How many more damn tests are you going to require?" yelled David Herzog. "We spent over one billion dollars on testing this year. We spent a billion dollars last year, and five hundred million the year before that! The data is there, Jane. And the test that *really* matters is us against the rest of the world, and right now we are losing that race by a mile."

"The situation really sucks," Derick Ernst pleaded. "If we don't act quickly, America will go from being the world's only superpower to being a half-assed banana republic. You, Jane, are going to be responsible for that demise."

"That's not fair at all. I am *not* the only one who objects to…"

"You are the leader of the flat-Earth movement!" Herzog interrupted. "You are the one who has stopped our progress and have ignored the scientific consensus at every turn."

Jane was fuming. "The only *consensus* is among those scientists who have a direct financial benefit in seeing their so-called-consensus implemented! It's like saying that all red-heads should be given one million dollars each because there is an overwhelming consensus amongst red-heads that this would be a good policy!"

David was done. "Jane, this paralysis-by-analysis needs to stop now!"

Jane sighed. "What exactly do you want me to do, Dave?"

"We need you to do the same thing that every other country on the Earth is already doing. We need to start catching up," Herzog stated. "For starters, we need to *mandate* that everyone gets the telomere gene modification."

"You want to *force* people to get the Old Age Gene fix?" Jane asked. "Aren't most Americans already getting that treatment anyway? Voluntarily?"

Ernst nodded his head, "Yes, but we need to make it mandatory."

"But how are you going to *force* grown adults to do this? You can't evict them from public schools the way we do with kids who don't get vaccines."

"No, but we can certainly take away their Medicare benefits. Hell, we'll take away their Social Security as well." Herzog stated emphatically.

Jane was stunned. "You're going to refuse to give seniors their Social Security, after they've paid into the system for 40 years?"

"Absolutely. We've already poll-tested it. A clear majority of U.S. citizens, at least the younger ones, are fully behind forcing their fellow citizens to get this treatment. It's for the common good. It reduces costs and improves outcomes for everyone."

Jane, stood up, arched her aching back and began pacing. "What else do you want to do?"

"We need to massively improve the American worker's productivity, so the Endurance and the Anti-Sloth gene therapies should also be required," answered Herzog.

"I hate that name 'Anti-Sloth Gene'," Ernst replied. "Why can't we call it the Work-a-holic gene or something like that. It would be more marketable."

Jane couldn't believe that Ernst was concerned about the *name* of a therapy. "It's doesn't matter what the hell you *call* it. What matters is the harm it could do in the long run."

"Jane, you can either hop on-board this train or you can let it run you over." Ernst responded.

"I may just jump in front of it!"

"Also, we plan to include the Strength Gene in the standard treatment. That will help with overall worker productivity, and it will also improve our military and our performance in sports," Herzog stated.

Jane put her hands over her face in frustration.

"Jane, I know that you think it's irrelevant and stupid, but you don't understand how important athletics are to national pride, and to the nation's performance in other areas. It's a snowball effect."

"Yay sports!" yelled Jane in a mocking tone as she rolled her eyes. "Any other mutations that you plan to force on your fellow citizens?"

"The Intelligence Gene will definitely be required," Herzog said matter-of-factly.

"Of course, it will!" Jane replied sarcastically. "To what level?"

David and Derick exchanged glances, "We were thinking of an IQ score somewhere around 170?"

"You want the *average* citizen to have an IQ in the range of Leonardo da Vinci and Albert Einstein? That's nuts!" exclaimed Jane.

"The intelligence gene only works well if it's administered shortly after birth. Some other countries started implementing it years ago, and their kids now appear to be in the 140 to 160 range. So, we need to exceed that level or we risk falling behind," Derick Ernst reasoned.

Jane was exasperated. "This is completely out of hand."

"We were also thinking that it would be a good idea to offer the American public options for a few of the 'beauty genes' at no charge, to encourage more participation in the program." Ernst added, "Blue eyes, high cheek bones, double eye lashes, maybe add three inches of height, harmless options like that."

"It's unbelievable to me that you can throw around terms like 'harmless' so matter-of-factly!" Jane exclaimed.

Ernst shrugged his shoulders, "They've all been tested on animals, and the double eye-lash gene enhancement has been on the market for years with no adverse effects."

"Nearly every other nation has already done it." Herzog reasoned.

Jane was tired of the same old arguments. There was no reasoning with these people.

"When is this all supposed happen?" she asked.

"We're introducing the legislation this week. President Fernstrom expects you to fully and enthusiastically support this bill every step of the way," Herzog answered.

"And if I don't?"

Herzog raised his eyebrows, "You serve at the pleasure of the President."

"Are you suggesting that I should submit a resignation letter to the President, just in case he wants to accept it?"

"That would be prudent."

Two days later, after only five months in office, the administration announced that Jane had resigned from her post to, "Spend more time with her family and to pursue other opportunities". President Fernstrom thanked Jane for her service to her country, accepted her resignation, and announced his choice to replace her the following day.

A CNN-sponsored poll taken in 2027 indicated that the American public's opinion of genetic modifications was 83% positive, similar to its overwhelming acceptance in other countries.

In addition to IVF (In Vitro Fertilization) genetic modifications, and treating nearly all infants at birth with genetic injections, the U.S. and other wealthy countries began adding the CRISPR viruses for endurance, strength and intelligence to their water supplies. This didn't work nearly as well as IVF treatments and injections at birth, but it did act as a booster, and it partially mutated those who had avoided treatments as embryos, or as infants.

Three months later, the World Court, at The Hague, released its landmark ruling titled *The International Mandate for Combating Genetic Privilege.* The court's ruling declared that genetic manipulation was giving citizens of wealthier countries an unfair *genetic privilege.* The ruling decreed that, in the interest of equality and social justice, wealthier countries, through the UN, would be required to provide genetic optimization therapies to the citizens of all third world countries, free of charge.

CHAPTER 24

Jane's New Start

January 20, 2027

"Oh, my goodness," Cindy exclaimed as she fawned over Jane's newborn baby Sarah. "She is absolutely beautiful."

"Thanks, Cindy!" Jane beamed as she rocked her two-week-old bundle of joy. "I have to admit, life is pretty good."

"Really?" Cindy was a bit shocked. "Four weeks ago, you had the ear of the president of the United States! Don't you miss being the head of a huge government agency? Don't you miss the power and the excitement?"

"Not one bit," Jane replied. "Once I had Sarah, none of that crap seemed important in the least. I already have more money than I'll ever be able spend. I don't need the power, I don't need the excitement, and I certainly don't need the headaches -- fighting tooth and nail, every day, with absolute idiots over every little thing. Old friends like you, however, that's something that I'll always need."

Jane and Cindy smiled at each other.

"Do you want to hold her?"

"I'd love to, but I probably shouldn't. I haven't been feeling very well lately."

Jane was somewhat relieved that Cindy had said "no" because she noticed that her long-time friend appeared to be a bit under the weather. Cindy still had those signature, amazingly thick, mascara-free eyelashes, but her eyes were now glassy and unfocused. Her skin looked rather gray, her movements were a bit unsteady, and she seemed to be constantly short of breath.

"Let me get you some coffee, or some juice, or something."

As Jane rose from her chair, holding baby Sarah in one arm, Cindy slowly started to get up as well.

"No Cindy," replied Jane. "I can get it, I've been sitting all day. I'll put Sarah in her bassinet."

Two years later, Jane and her friends would have streams of mascara running down their cheeks as they cried at Cindy's funeral. At the young age of only twenty-six, she would succumb to pneumonia after a struggle with coronary heart disease. Unfortunately, it would take another decade for scientists to connect all the dots as to why this had happened.

Cindy wasn't the only human with double eyelashes. In fact, the legendary actress Liz Taylor, had the same genetic mutation. Their beautiful lashes may have had everyone else drooling in envy, but there was a catch. It was a genetic transcription oddity, in the sixteenth chromosome, that created those double eyelashes for Liz Taylor, Cindy and many others. Unfortunately, that double eyelash mutation also gave people a ten-times higher propensity to suffer from heart disease. The malady that led to the demise of both Liz Taylor, and Jane's best friend, Cindy.

Decades later it was determined that the CRISPR-created 'beauty gene' double-eyelash modification had contributed to nearly one hundred million premature deaths, which, in turn, would result in over one-trillion dollars in law suits awards.

CHAPTER 25

The Curse of Underachieving

September 20, 2040

Jane and her now 13-year-old daughter, Sarah, had settled in Carlisle, Pennsylvania, a small town about eighty miles west of Philadelphia. Jane had fallen in love with the area during her stint at the University of Pennsylvania, but unfortunately, life was not as ideal as she hoped for her little girl.

It was early in the new school year and, once again, Sarah was running home from the bus-stop crying. Jane wrapped Sarah in a big hug and walked her into the house. She wiped the tears from Sarah's cheeks as they sat on the living room couch.

"What happened today, honey?" Jane asked, even though she was pretty sure that she already knew the answer.

"You don't understand, Mom. I'm the only one. I'm stupid, I'm weak, and I'm slow. Everyone makes fun of me all day long. It never stops. I feel so alone." Sarah was now sobbing uncontrollably. She was only able to speak one or two words between every breath, gasping desperately for air with every other word.

"It's ok, Sarah." Jane held her daughter tight, petting her hair, "It's going to be okay."

"No, it's not!" screamed Sarah. "It's never going to get better, it's only going to get worse."

"Don't say that, sweetie. You have to be positive!"

"I love you, Mom, but you have no idea what I am going through. You were smart! You were popular! You played sports! You got to be everything that I'm not!"

"I'm so sorry. I'll go to your school to talk to your teachers tomorrow. I'll try to straighten this out."

"That won't do anything! Please, let me go with Marybeth. When I'm with them, it's the only time that I'm happy. They understand me!"

Now Jane was crying too. She decided to bring up the unmentionable.

"Sarah, you're only 13 years old. You're still young enough to get the gene treatments. You could still get some of the benefit from them, I could set you up with…"

"No, Mom! That would make me a mutant, too. I want to get away from them, not become one of them! I want to live with Sister Marybeth and her family. I want to be a Stauffer Mennonite."

Jane tried to change the subject. "Have they let you out of Special Ed for math yet?"

"No, and they never will, because I only have an IQ of 125."

"You know, Sarah, 20 years ago, you'd be one of the smartest kids in the school."

"But it's *not* 20 years ago, Mom! Today, everyone else in my school has an artificial IQ of 150 or higher, which means that I'm the dumbest kid in the school. They *all* make fun of me. Even the teachers!"

"I'm so sorry, honey." Jane embraced her daughter and gave her a kiss on her head. "Let's go for a run! That should help get your mind off your troubles."

"Why even bother? My mile time yesterday was 6:10."

"Sarah, that is an amazing time for a 13-year-old!"

Sarah shook her head in despair. "No, it's horrible. I'm the slowest person in my class and not just by a little. Everyone else runs their mile in like four minutes. They all finish a lap and a half ahead of me. Today, Joey ran a 3:57."

Jane didn't know what to do. "We'll find some sport for you to play."

Sarah was crying uncontrollably. "No, we won't! I talked to Coach Kammerer today and he told me that the school board has decided that untreated students like me won't be allowed to play competitive sports because there's too much risk of us getting hurt. He called me a liability."

Sarah looked at her mother and put her hands together, pleading through her tears, "Mom, I am begging you. Please let me go live with MaryBeth!"

CHAPTER 26

Life as a Mennonite

June 2, 2044

Jane was despondent when she finally folded and gave Sarah permission to move to the Stauffer Mennonite village. She tried to maintain a stiff upper lip. Jane knew that letting her little girl live with her friend Marybeth and the Mennonites was the only thing that would make Sarah happy -- and happy she was.

Followers of the Mennonite faith are a rather conservative bunch, but the Stauffer Mennonites were ultra-conservative, even by Mennonite standards. They were a small group, maybe 4,000 members total, scattered amongst a few rural communities throughout the country. There were a several Stauffer Mennonite villages in Lancaster and Snyder Counties in Pennsylvania, two in St. Mary's County in Maryland, and one in Dallas County in Missouri. Sarah loved her new life in the village. The community didn't allow genetic enhancements of any kind. As a result, Sarah didn't just fit in, she absolutely thrived. Sarah finally found joy, living a life where she was no longer below average. Now, in many ways, she was slightly *above* average.

For the first two years, Jane tried to visit Sarah at least once a month. The Mennonites were kind to Jane. They did nothing overtly to make her feel unwelcomed, at least not at first, but it was clear that she wasn't one of them. On the sidewalks of the village, happy conversations would suddenly stop whenever Jane approached, even when she was with Sarah.

Three years after arriving, Sarah began courting a fine young man named Jonah, who was MaryBeth's second cousin. It had taken Jane months to become accustom to the term *courting* instead of *dating*. The Mennonites perceived a very significant difference between these two expressions. They found the term *dating* to be rather vulgar.

"How are you feeling, Mom?" asked Sarah.

Jane, looked over at her little girl who had now blossomed into a 17-year-old beautiful young woman with brunette hair and gorgeous blue eyes. Jane always looked forward to visiting Sarah, but today's meeting would be a bit more stressful. On this trip, Jane had been invited to Jonah's house to meet his family.

"I couldn't be more excited!" Jane said with a smile, hoping to mask her worries.

Jonah's parents, along with his seven brothers and sisters, lived on a beautiful 650-acre farm three miles outside of the village. Jonah's father, Elijah, had built the family's 2,500-square-foot home and adjacent barn with his own hands some twenty years ago. The home was constructed from boulders and timber harvested from Elijah's own property. The logs were cut into lumber, precisely to his specifications, at the village's Mennonite-owned sawmill. As was common amongst the Mennonites, Elijah had paid via barter, letting the mill keep 25% of the wood in return for their services. The home was perched on a small hill in the middle of the family's property, overlooking vegetable gardens, corn fields, pastures filled with dairy cows, and a stream that meandered through the valley below. The scene would have made a spectacular postcard.

Jane and Sarah climbed the wooden steps to the home's massive wrap-around porch. As they reached the top of the stairs they were greeted by Elijah and his wife, Vera. Their son, Jonah, stood silently behind them.

"Welcome to our home Mrs..…." Vera paused and shook her head, "I mean Miss Stewart. It is a pleasure to finally meet you. Sarah has told us so much about you."

"Likewise. Your farm is truly spectacular!" replied Jane.

"Thank you so much. Please come in," said Jonah's mother, obviously, a bit nervous. Vera led everyone into the living room.

Vera gestured towards Jane, "Here. Let me take your coat." There was an uncomfortable pause. "Oh, how silly of me. You aren't wearing a coat! I'm sorry. I'm just very…"

"She's a bit flustered" injected Elijah. "She knows that city-folk like yourself aren't as familiar with our simpler way of life. That you are accustomed to much fancier things. She's been working like a plow-horse all week trying to fancy the place up for you."

Vera stared at the floor with her hands folded in front of her.

"That's so kind of you, Vera. Your home is immaculate and whatever you are cooking smells divine!" Jane smiled, but Vera continued to look uneasy.

Jane continued. "I must admit that I've been pretty nervous myself. I'm so excited to finally meet the family of the man my daughter adores. It brings me such comfort, knowing that she's in good hands."

Feeling that it was a sweet moment Jane instinctively stepped forward to give Jonah's mother a hug, but Vera immediately backed away. Jane then returned to her original spot. This awkward interaction was followed by another very long, very uncomfortable pause. Jane made a mental note to herself that Mennonites, apparently, were not 'huggers'.

Vera stammered, "Dinner should be almost ready. I... I should go check on it."

Jane started to rise from the couch, "Could you use some help?"

"No, please, no!" Vera put out her hands, "You're our guest. Just sit here with everyone and talk. Yes, you all talk. That would be nice."

Vera shuffled off to the kitchen while staring at the floor, shaking her head and mumbling something to herself as she went.

Jane sat on one couch with her daughter Sarah next to her. Jonah and his father sat on the other couch facing them. They just stared at each other in silence. Not sure what to say. Uncomfortable, Jane looked around the room and took note that it seemed a bit eerie. The room contained only furniture. There were no flat screen TVs; there was no stereo; there were no gaming systems, pictures, or even electric clocks.

"The Lord made a fine day for us today, didn't he?" stated Elijah.

"Yes. It's a beautiful day indeed," replied Jane with a big smile. "You truly have a little piece of paradise here."

Elijah nodded his head and there was yet another long stretch of silence. Jane's head started spinning, thinking about what they could safely talk about. What do Mennonites even discuss in their downtime – Corn? Horses? Chinch bugs?

Elijah cleared his throat. "Sarah, tells us that you are in the process of going back to university to become a doctor?"

"Yes, I am. I already have a PhD, but now I'm studying to get my M.D. Returning to college at thirty-eight has been quite the transition."

"So, now you will be a *real* doctor?"

"Well, yes. I will be a medical doctor. Yes…"

Once again, the room fell into silence. A slight breeze wafted through the home. You could hear a pin drop.

"It's so nice to finally meet you," mumbled Jane, again, not sure what else to say.

"Likewise, however, we are doing things a bit backwards, aren't we?" huffed Elijah. "Very irregular indeed."

Sarah and Jonah squirmed uneasily, knowing exactly what Elijah meant. Jane, on the other hand, had absolutely no clue what Elijah was referring to, but then, everything about the Mennonites seemed a bit "irregular" to her.

"I'm sorry, Elijah, I'm not following?"

"Vera and I -- and you and Sarah's father – Why isn't he here? We *all* should have discussed and arranged this entire courtship in advance. This is *not* the proper way to do things. Not proper at all."

Jane scoffed and was about to give Elijah a piece of her mind, but then she looked over at her daughter who was staring at her pleadingly. As much as she wanted to defend herself, nothing was more important to her than her baby girl's happiness.

"I sincerely apologize if the absence Sarah's father in our lives does not reflect your Mennonite beliefs. I hope that you can see it in your heart to not let this irregularity taint your view of Sarah, or jeopardize the courtship between Sarah and your son."

Jane, Sarah, and Jonah all stared at Elijah intently as he sat stoically, stroking his long graying beard.

"Please excuse me for a moment." Elijah stood up, "I'm going to see if my wife needs any help in the kitchen."

Elijah's son, Jonah, accidentally allowed a chuckle to escape from his lips. This elicited a stern growl from his father. Jonah quickly sobered his face and averted his eyes to the floor, avoiding his father's angry stare. Elijah stomped off towards the kitchen in a huff.

When his father was out of earshot, Jonah finally spoke. "I'm sorry for laughing, Ms. Stewart. It's just that, in my entire life, I don't think I've ever seen my father choose to be in a kitchen while food was being prepared!"

Jane let out an exasperated sigh. This was going to be an interesting dinner.

CHAPTER 27

The Wedding

May 13, 2046

Two years later, Jane was standing in the narthex of the Mennonite chapel waiting to walk 19-year-old Sarah, her only child, down the aisle to be married. Jane had only been able, or allowed, to visit Sarah three times in the past two years. This was partially due to Jane being busy completing her residency. The Mennonites, however, had made it subtlety, but abundantly clear that it would be best if Jane's visits were short and seldom. The same message had been sent to Sarah's previous friends from outside the Mennonite community. As a result, the bride's side of the chapel was virtually empty, while the groom's side was packed.

"Are you ready?" asked Jane.

"Of course, I am! Don't worry Momma. The good Lord has brought Jonah and me together. This was meant to be!"

Sarah was smiling from ear to ear. Even in her plain and modest white dress, she was radiant.

"Before we take this walk, I have something to give to you," Jane said as she pulled a white, pearl-embroidered handkerchief out of her purse and handed it to her daughter.

"Mom…" Sarah softly responded as she gazed at the keepsake.

"The pearls were your great grandma Sandy's. I know that you're not allowed to have jewelry or have anything flashy, but I still wanted you to have this. You can keep it in a drawer and look at it now and then to remember us."

"Thank you, Mom. It's beautiful."

Jane reached out and held her daughter's face in her hands, trying to drink-in every last drop of this fleeting moment. Jane wanted to cement this instant of time into her memory forever.

"Sarah, I love you more than anything on this earth. You know that, don't you?"

"Yes, Momma."

"Letting go of you was, and still is, the hardest thing that I've ever had to do in my entire life," Jane caught her breath, trying to hold back the tears. "But seeing you here today, truly happy, and about to marry the man you love. This makes it all worthwhile."

"I love you, Mom." Sarah wrapped her mother in a tight hug and whispered in her ear, "Thank you for giving me everything I ever wanted."

Jane held her daughter until an obviously-intentional cough interrupted their moment.

"They're ready for you, sister," a Mennonite woman urged Sarah.

Jane smiled. "Come on, kid. Let's get you married-off!"

Jane and Sarah composed themselves, took a deep breath in unison, and headed down the aisle. Jane wanted their walk to last forever, but in what seemed like a mere instant, they had reached the alter where the pastor and Jonah were standing.

"Who gives this woman to this man?" asked the preacher.

"I do" replied Jane. And then it was over. Jane left her daughter at the altar and took a seat, by herself, in the front pew of the barely-occupied left side of the chapel.

For Jane, the remainder of the wedding ceremony was a blur. She found it very difficult to concentrate. Her mind kept flashing back to all those memories of Sarah growing up - the good times, the bad times, the *potential* parenting mistakes, and the *undeniable* parenting mistakes that she had made along the way. She couldn't help but think of all the things that she could have done differently, if only she could go back in time.

Jane's attention was temporarily redirected as the minister referred to Genesis 2:24, "...And here the Lord instructs that we should leave our parents and cleave to our spouse and become one with them."

Jane felt the eyes of the pastor, and seemingly the entire congregation, glaring at her, the harlot mother of the bride. This struck a nerve with her. Jane certainly was no biblical scholar, but she did know that Genesis 2:24 referred to the requirement that the *man* was leave his parents and cleave to his wife. The *man* was the one who was supposed to be "leaving and cleaving", not her baby Sarah! While Jonah seemed like a wonderful guy, Jane certainly did not feel as though she was gaining a son. This was not a fair trade at all!

None of this was fair! A stream of tears dribbled down Jane's cheek as reality set in. She was officially losing a daughter, her only child.

The reception dinner was held outside, in a grassy field, which was conveniently nestled between the chapel and the congregation's cemetery.

"How handy," Jane mumbled to herself. "Everything you need from the womb to the tomb -- in a plot the size of a football field."

Jane was seated at a table with seven of Sarah's unmarried female acquaintances from the Mennonite community. Jane had met a few of them previously, but didn't really know any of them well enough to engage in any meaningful conversation. Jane listened to Sarah's friends rant for a good thirty minutes about a variety of mundane subjects, and conspiracy theories -- including the evils of childhood vaccinations. As much as she felt the urge to educate the ladies with a dose of medical science, she decided that it would be wiser to keep her knowledge to herself. As she sipped her apple cider at this dry gathering, all she could think about was how badly she needed a drink. Not a beer. She needed a couple flaming shots of Jägermeister... maybe three or four. Jane glanced over at Sarah, sitting at the head table. Her daughter certainly *seemed* to be incredibly happy.

Suddenly, a bustling panic consumed the reception. Over the cacophony of Mennonite voices Jane thought that she heard the faint clanging of a bell coming out of the east, miles in the distance. Ten seconds later she heard another bell, much clearer, this one less than a mile away. Chairs were overturned, small children were scooped up in the arms of their parents and older siblings. A third bell clanged, this one from a farmhouse directly across the road from the chapel. The wedding guests grabbed as much food as they could carry from the tables.

One of the elders nearly knocked Jane over as he dove for a large hand bell mounted on the wall of the chapel and began ringing it with exuberance.

"Move with haste into the haven of the chapel, brothers and sisters! – Ensure that your children are with you and don your masks."

Jane, seeing no reason to run while wearing her Sunday best, was one of the last to climb the stairs of the church. As she approached the large wooden doors she heard what sounded like the engine of a small, single engine aircraft, far in the distance. She started to turn around, but was roughly pushed into the church by an elder as the heavy door slammed shut behind her.

"Please put these on Ma'am", requested the elder as he handed her a medical mask and some sort of veil. Jane quickly put on the mask and squeezed the nose-clip to seal it, a task that she had performed thousands of times during her residency. She had no clue, however, why she was doing this at her daughter's wedding. Jane looked around the church and took note of the semi-organized chaos. While children cried in fear, some of the adults wrapped the food trays in waxed paper while others bolted the windows.

"Brothers and Sisters, please gather near the center of the building!" implored the elders.

Jane could hear the plane getting closer as she walked over to Sarah.

"What's this all about, honey? And how the *hell* am I supposed to wear this *damn* veil thing?" asked Jane.

"Mother!" snapped Sarah. "You are in the Lord's house!"

Jane rolled her eyes. "I'm sorry. I'm a bit stressed out. What's going on?"

Sarah sighed, stood up, and adjusted the veil over her mother's head, "Didn't you participate in our any of drills during your visits?"

"No, Sarah, I didn't. They must have planned the drills during the 360 days of the year that I was *not* allowed to visit my only child," chided Jane with obvious sarcasm.

"Point taken," admitted Sarah with a smile.

"Take cover!" shouted an elder.

The plane was much closer now. Sarah grabbed Jane's hand and pulled her down so that they were both kneeling behind a pew next to her new husband Jonah.

"Why do we need to take cover? Who's out there?" asked Jane.

"We are one of only a few communities left in America, maybe in the world, whose kids haven't been genetically re-engineered. So, we have to take every precaution," Sarah replied.

"I thought that you had all of your bases covered. No vaccines, you grow your own food, and you totally control your water supply."

"Exactly," stated Jonah. "So, the only other way that the government could force those genetic mutations on us would be through aerial spraying."

Jane shook her head. "You all don't believe in that 'chemtrails' conspiracy crap, do you? Those white lines that you see in the sky are *contrails* made from frozen water. They are *not* clouds of mysterious chemicals. Jet fuel molecules are made from strings of carbon and hydrogen, so when the fuel burns it turns into carbon-dioxide and water. At 35,000 feet, the air is very cold, something like negative 50 degrees, even in the middle of summer. So the water vapor immediately turns into billions of tiny ice crystals…"

"Mom," Sarah interrupted and laughed. "We're not stupid. We know that chem-trails are crazy-talk -- for dozens of reasons. With the jet stream blowing at 100 miles per hour, chemicals released at 35,000 feet could land anywhere. Spraying us with chemicals from airliners would be insane."

Jane smiled. Her daughter was one smart cookie. Maybe she had done a decent job of raising her after all.

Jonah continued. "What we *are* worried about, though, is the government using helicopters and low-flying crop-duster aircraft to deliver gene-altering drugs to our children. Since most of us don't have phones, we've set up this bell-ringing warning system."

At that moment, they heard the plane fly directly over the church, not more than 100 feet above the steeple.

An elder yelled, "It's a duster! Make sure that the young ones are fully covered!"

Cletus laughed as he buzzed the steeple of the Mennonite chapel in his 1941 Stearman 450 Crop Duster. Even at 103 years of age, the bi-plane was a beautiful aircraft. Its candy apple red paintjob glistened brilliantly in the clear blue sky.

Cletus was returning from a crop dusting job at the 2,000 acre Williamson soybean farm, twenty miles north of the chapel. Ten minutes prior to this, Cletus had completed dumping 400-gallons of the pesticide *Asana* on the Williamson farm, to control a nasty infestation of green stink bugs,

His shortest return trip to the Snyder County airport would have taken him nowhere near the quiet Mennonite village, but Cletus was an ass. He had some extra fuel in his tank. He couldn't imagine a more enjoyable way to burn it than by taking a detour and watching some stupid Mennonites scramble.

"Run like hell, you morons!" yelled Cletus. "That's right. I'm a CIA secret agent sent here to gas your paranoid, bible-thumping Mennonite asses! Maybe if y'all had a little genetic engineering you wouldn't be so damn soft in the head!"

Thoroughly pleased with himself, Cletus banked his plane to the south and headed back to the airport.

Thirty minutes after the plane passed, the elders gave the all-clear for the parishioners to leave the church. Their first task was to grab some trash cans and dispose of any food that had been left outside.

As Sarah exited the church, the first thing she noticed was her wedding cake. Amidst the disarray, no one had bothered to bring it inside. She knew that it would have to be thrown away immediately to ensure that no child would eat it. It was a beautiful cake. Sarah had baked it and decorated herself. It was her gift to her guests, but now, it was toxic waste. Sarah sat on the church steps and began to cry.

CHAPTER 28

Médecins Sans Frontières

February 3, 2047

Eight months following her close brush with Mennonite Armageddon, at her daughter Sarah's wedding, Jane completed her residency at the Mayo Clinic in Rochester, Minnesota.

Jane was now a multi-millionaire, who had just graduated at the top of her class, from the number one teaching hospital in the nation. She had already published a litany of top-notch research papers, and held several dozen lucrative patents. Naturally, she was courted by the best hospitals, research organizations and universities throughout the U.S. and Europe.

Jane mulled her choices, realizing that she was once again free to do almost anything, or to go virtually anywhere that she pleased. Her daughter was married-off with no phone or email access. Their only means of communication was through snail mail -- letters made from dead trees sent through the U.S. Postal Service, which had become an archaic art to say the least. On top of that, Jane did *not* have a man that she needed to worry about. She tried to remember the last date she had been on and drew a complete blank. It had been a very long time.

Doing genetic research would keep Jane challenged and she was certainly good at it, but she had already been down that road several times. She wanted to try something different with the next phase of her life. She craved the satisfaction of helping people directly. To most, this would have seemed like a huge step backwards, but what Jane really wanted to do was open a private practice. She yearned to be a general practitioner. The big question was, where should she hang her shingle? On Rodeo Drive? In Beverley Hills? Or maybe in the mountains of Appalachia?

Jane picked up her cell phone and dialed a friend of her father's, Dr. David Butterly. Dr. Dave was formerly the Dean of Medicine at Duke University. He now sat on the board of Doctors Without Borders, aka *Médecins Sans Frontières* or *MSF*.

"Jane! Long time, no see. How are you doing? How's your dad?"

"Dad's doing great, Dave. He's loving retirement. And I just wrapped up my residency. So, I wanted to call you to let you know that I was thinking of possibly spending a year or two with MSF."

"Wow, that's great," replied Dr. Butterly, enthusiastically. "We'd love to have you on our board of directors!"

Jane laughed, "No, Dave. Thanks for the offer, but I have no interest in serving on your board. I already sit on way too many boards as it is."

"Oh … okay," Dave was confused. "So, what do you want to do, Jane? I can probably swing you into any gig you want."

"Well, you tell me. What's the toughest job that you have? The one that you have the hardest time filling?"

"You mean, field work?" Dave paused for a moment. "You're asking me what MSF's toughest field job is?"

"Yes, sir!"

"Pardon my French, Jane, but those would be what we at *Médecins Sans Frontières* affectionally refer to as our *bat merde fou*, or 'bat shit crazy' assignments. The ones that are in austere and highly dangerous locations."

"Alright. So, give me an example."

"Like -- I don't know -- general practitioner work at a tiny two-person clinic in some remote village located in a terrorist-infested, war-torn nation with little or no governance."

"Sounds peachy to me!" Jane responded.

"No offense, but we generally don't send women on those sorts of assignments."

Jane quipped, "So, are you saying that you have plenty of male doctors volunteering for those assignments? And, *all* of those slots are already filled? There's no room for even one token *girl* like me?"

Dr. Butterly laughed. "No, Jane. They aren't *all* filled. In fact, virtually none of them are filled. You can have your pick of the litter. And even if they were all filled, I'd sure as hell make room for you, one of the smartest humans on the planet, to do whatever crazy-ass job you want to do for us. But, there are serious risks to be considered when it comes to these regions. I'm not only talking about the lack of clean water, nasty parasites, and malaria. I'm talking about the real possibility of assault, rape, murder – you name it."

"I'll carry mace."

"We've had doctors kidnapped and forced at gunpoint to go to the front lines and provide medical services to terrorists while under fire. It's not pretty."

"Dave, I appreciate your concern, but you're not going to talk me out of this. And, my dad doesn't have to ever know that this conversation took place. You don't have to worry about him. So, why don't you save us both some time and just tell me the assignment you have which is the hardest to fill? That's the one I'd prefer."

Dr. Butterly's reply was a single word. *"Terekeka!"*

CHAPTER 29

Terekeka

April 21, 2047

Jane walked briskly towards the grass-thatch and mud medical hut. The pre-dawn African sky glowed with beautiful shades of red and orange, mostly due to the tons of dust that hung permanently in the air. A line of several dozen people had already gathered outside the hut, seeking medical attention. Some were standing, most were sitting or lying in the dirt.

Terekeka was a hamlet in South Sudan, about fifty miles north of the capital city of Juba. Like the rest of the country, Terekeka had been impoverished and torn by violence for decades. But this small village did have one odd, rather unique claim to fame. In the year 2019, GammaTek Labs, Inc., a pioneer in the field of genetic engineering, had selected Terekeka for the initial human trials of its "Big Five" gene-modification regimen. The Big Five had included the strength, intelligence, endurance, work-a-holic, and anti-aging genes.

In addition to the Big Five, GammaTek had also randomly included beauty-gene modifications in some of the doses. These included the blue eye gene and/or the double eye-lash gene. Terekeka's citizens had been rewarded handsomely for their participation in these tests, receiving the equivalent of three year's salary for allowing each of their children, ten years of age or younger, to receive GammaTek's CRISPR-created concoctions.

This drug-testing tactic was not abnormal. Pharmaceutical companies often performed their initial trials in third world countries, primarily because it was easier, and cheaper, to recruit volunteers. There was also less liability risk if something were to go awry. This pleased the corporate lawyers, which was always a good thing.

Non-scientists often wonder why so many biological studies are done on fruit flies. Budgetary watch-dog-groups regularly site fruit fry research as prime examples of government waste, but nothing could be further from the truth. Fruit fly studies are extremely valuable because fruit flies have a very short life-cycle and gestation period – on the order of a few weeks. This means that the effect of a drug, chemical, or gene, can be studied over three or four generations in only a few months. Of course, humans aren't fruit flies, so the testing done on these insects, while valuable, does not always apply to humans.

Back in 2019, GammaTek desperately needed a human version of fruit flies for their Phase III trials of the Big Five therapy. Their goal was to find a village with one of the fastest generational turn-overs on Earth. This search led GammaTek to the village of Terekeka.

GammaTek's results were spectacular, at least from a clinical and scientific point of view. Following the treatments, there were no reported deaths or even minor illnesses. Five years later, Terekeka's genetically-treated children had tested well above the untreated children in nearby villages in terms of IQ, strength, and endurance. Better yet, GammaTek had included a gene-drive feature in all the treatments, so any future offspring of the treated children would also exhibit extraordinary IQ's, strength, and endurance.

Unfortunately, in terms of the more socially-important metrics, such as crime, per-capita gross domestic product (GDP), and poverty levels, there had been virtually no improvement in Terekeka. It was generally the same impoverished, crime infested village that it had always been.

"Wilujeng énjing!" Jane exclaimed to her small medical team as she entered the hut, practicing her limited Sudanese language skills.

"And a very good morning to you as well, Dr. Jane," replied Jane's assistant, Dr. Sumaya Keji, who was already hard at work treating patients. Sumaya was a brilliant, 27-year-old native of Terekeka. Her IQ was somewhere in the neighborhood of 180. She had left the village of Terekeka at 13 years of age to study in the U.S., where she remained throughout medical school. After completing her residency, Sumaya had returned to Terekeka with the noble goal of making a difference; to make her home a better, healthier and happier place.

"How's your day going so far, Dr. Sumaya?" Jane inquired as she scrubbed-down.

"Same as always, Dr. Jane. Parasites and pregnancies, followed closely by more parasites and additional pregnancies."

"And how old are our expectant mothers today?"

"Twelve and thirteen," replied Sumaya shaking her head in disgust, "But their 40-year-old husbands are ecstatic, so we've got that going for us!"

The taking of child brides, usually without the consent of the bride herself, is a common-place practice/problem throughout Africa. It is estimated that 20 million of these children are forced into marriages every year. Social science theory often blames this custom on poverty and lack of education. This is why GammaTek's Phase III trial prospectuses predicted that the *Big Five* CRISPR cocktail would swiftly lift the entire village of Terekeka out of poverty, solve the child bride issue, and a plethora of other so-called third-world problems in the process.

Unfortunately, although GammaTek's CRISPR-enabled mutations accomplished all their physical goals, they didn't accomplish any of their social objectives. The measured IQs of Terekeka treated citizens (and their descendants) increased significantly, but those higher IQs were almost never fully utilized or developed. The girls in the village were still only allowed to attend school until the age of nine or ten. Only 9% finished primary school, and fewer than 3% went on to high school. The other genetic advantages also seemed to be wasted. The strength and endurance improvements, instead of being used to produce more goods and services, were used to engage in more battles with other villages. The beauty gene in some of the young girls, combined with the enhanced endurance gene in the older men, actually made the child bride problem worse.

Jane finished scrubbing and called for the next patient in line. She was a12-year-old girl named Iklas, who was accompanied by her clearly, middle-aged husband, named Kamal.

"What seems to be the problem, young lady?" asked Jane, intentionally directing the question towards Iklas.

The interpreter asked the question to the young, blue-eyed, African girl, but it was her husband Kamal who answered.

"He says that they have been married for six months and that she still is not pregnant. He wants to know if you have been giving her birth control pills."

Jane scoffed. If there was ever a place on Earth that was sorely in need of a boat-load of birth control pills, it was the village of Terekeka. Prior to the genetic modifications, its birth rate had been abnormally high compared to the rest of the planet, but after receiving the *Big Five* treatment, the birth rate had exploded. The exact reasons were unclear. Some researchers thought that it was due to the men or women, or both, being more fertile. Others insisted that it was because people with more endurance tend to have more sex. In any case, the result was that any married woman of childbearing age going six months without becoming pregnant was now a rare event.

"Tell Kamal that neither I, nor anyone else in this clinic have given this *child* any birth control pills. However, because she is only twelve, she is not old enough to safely have a child. So, I, and any other ethical medical doctor, would highly recommend that *both* you and she *should* be using birth control, or, preferably, abstinence."

If it were up to Jane, she would have been handing out birth control pills to any village girl who wanted them, but MSF forbade them from doing so unless the husband approved. The logic behind this rule was that handing out pills behind the backs of the husbands would only result in getting the MSF clinic getting kicked out of the village, which would be even worse for the girls.

Kamal was now screaming, but the translator remained calm. "He says that his family gave up thirty-two cows for her. Trading that many cows for a wife who bears no babies is not acceptable. He says that it's like stealing. He says that if you aren't giving her birth control then you need to fix her so that she can have babies."

The going rate for a wife in South Sudan ranges from around ten cows on the low end, up to forty or fifty cows on the high end. So, Iklas' price of thirty-two cows was near the average.

The interpreter continued, "He is saying that all of his other wives had children by this age, so the problem isn't him." Kamal continued screaming, the interpreter shook her head. "And now he's just screaming 'fix her, fix her' over and over."

Meanwhile, Kamal's child bride, Iklas, silently stared at the floor. A single tear streamed down her cheek.

"Come with me," demanded Jane as she grabbed Iklas' hand. "And you better stay right there!" she ordered, raising her voice and pointing her finger at Kamal who had taken one step to follow them. He didn't need a translator to know that it would be best for him to take a seat. The interpreter followed Jane into the examination room, which was really nothing more than a table and a chair, surrounded by a thin white curtain.

"Ask her where she got those," inquired Jane, pointing to bruises and lacerations on the young girl's arms and face.

The interpreter replied, "She says that she's not sure. She thinks that she got them while working in her garden."

Jane stood for a minute and stared at this poor child, wondering what to do. The girl then said something in Sudanese.

"She is asking why you're not fixing her," explained the interpreter. This broke Jane's heart.

Jane tried to maintain her composure as she responded. "First, you need to tell her that she does not need *fixing*. Then tell her that if she wants, I'm more than willing to tell her idiot husband..." Jane sighed and shook her head, "Obviously don't use that phrase, but tell her I can tell Kamal that she's infertile if that will convince him to return Iklas to her parents, if that's what she wants."

Iklas began crying and responded through the interpreter. "She says no. Her parents have already sold twenty-five of those cows and used the money to buy a house for her brother and his new bride. If she goes back home, her parents will be required to return those cows, which they no longer have. It will destroy her family."

There was a commotion outside the examination room. Kamal ripped open the curtain and confronted Jane and screamed, *"Naon anu salah? Naha pamajikan abdi nangis."* Jane understood enough Sudanese to know that Kamal was saying something along the lines of, "What is wrong? Why is my wife crying?" She also knew enough broken Sudanese to reply, *"Manéhna nu keur nangis lantaran anjeun hiji burit!"* Which roughly translates to, "She's crying because you are an ass."

Jane grabbed Kamal by his shirt, threw him out of the examination room, and tossed him to the floor. She glared at him and re-closed the curtain.

CHAPTER 30

Dinner and a Clue

April 21, 2047

Sumaya and Jane were having dinner in the kitchen of Jane's home in Terekeka. The house was Spartan by Western standards, but luxurious compared to the mud huts surrounding it. It had been another 11-hour work-day for Jane and a 14-hour day for her assistant Sumaya. Jane felt worn to the bone, but Sumaya was still as chipper as she had been at 4am that morning, when she arrived at the clinic.

"I don't know how you do it!" Jane exclaimed.

Sumaya smiled, "Well, I do have a few artificial genetic advantages which you lack."

"And you have certainly made the most of them." Jane toasted as they clinked their bottles of lukewarm cola.

"It's so disappointing that Terekeka isn't booming. The average IQ here is nearly at the genius level, but still, they are all just..." Jane was obviously flustered.

Sumaya grinned, "Stuck in their third-world existence?"

"Yes, exactly."

"Well Jane, I've spent fifteen years living in the third-world and twelve years living in the first-world. What I can tell you from my experience is that no amount genetic modification will ever improve a society unless that society's culture changes as well."

"But that doesn't work either, does it?" asked Jane. "The English, the French and the Dutch -- they all tried to change the culture three or four hundred years ago with their colonization efforts. The results were ineffective at best, and disastrous at worst."

"But they were outsiders! This is where I was born, right here in this village. My hope was that, since I came from the same roots as these people, that they would trust and listen to me!" Sumaya exclaimed. Then she sighed as a forlorn look shown in her eyes. "But I have to admit that the whole situation is starting to feel futile and hopeless."

"No way, Sumaya. *You* are doing great work here. The girls all love you. They look up to you. Not only are you helping them, but you're also their role model."

"Maybe. But what good does is it do when they're all married-off at eleven years of age? Sometimes I think that they were better off when they didn't know that other options existed. Ignorance is bliss?"

Jane nodded. "I know the feeling."

"Hopefully we can do *some* good," Sumaya stated. "You know that little girl, Iklas that you saw today?"

"Did MFS already find out that I man-handled her husband?" Jane asked.

Sumaya laughed, "No. At least, not that I know of! But I have noticed that, in the last year or so, a lot of these younger brides don't seem to be getting pregnant quite as often as they used to."

There was a brief pause as Jane squinted inquisitively at her colleague, "Are you giving those girls birth control pills?"

"No!"

"Because my lips are sealed if you are! Our fearless leaders back at MFS headquarters wouldn't be happy, but I won't say anything! Hell, I'll give you a damn medal."

"No, Jane, I'm not giving out birth control pills!"

"Okay, so Depo shots? Implants?"

Both women started laughing.

"Read my lips - I'm not giving out *any* birth control, of *any* kind, to *anyone*! It's against the rules, Jane. Unlike you, I am not richer than God, and I need this job!" Sumaya exclaimed.

"Fine, fine. I guess I'll believe you!" Jane smiled as she took a large gulp of her soda.

"You've read the GammaTek fertility reports, right?" Sumaya asked.

"Sure," Jane shrugged. "Everyone expected Terekeka's birth rates to decrease after the treatments, but instead, birth rates increased, both for those who were treated and their descendants."

"Right," replied Sumaya. "But the GammaTek report only includes data from the twenty-year period following the original genetic modifications."

"Which ended five years ago."

"Exactly! So, knowing that, I decided to pull the village records from the past five years."

"Are you sure the records are accurate?" asked Jane.

"Yes. After working with GammaTek's statisticians for twenty years, they picked-up some good best-practices. I'd say they're accurate to 1% or so."

Jane raised her eyebrows, "Impressive. And what do they show?"

"What they *seem* to indicate is that, over the past two or three years, birth rates have slowed. And, in the past 12 months, the slowing has accelerated."

"Maybe the citizens of Terekeka are finally understanding that having a dozen kids isn't necessary for financial prosperity?"

Sumaya scoffed and shook her head, "I don't think so, Jane. Look at what happened today at the clinic. There is no way that we're suddenly being hit with an epidemic of village-wide enlightenment."

"Okay. So, what do you think *is* going on? What's your next step?" Jane asked.

"Funny you should ask!" Sumaya smiled and began rummaging through her briefcase. Beamed with excitement, she pulled out a twenty-page research plan and handed it to Jane. Sumaya continued, "First, I would like to verify that these birth rates really are dropping. It certainly seems to be the case, but I want to make sure."

"And after you confirm that they really are dropping?"

"Obviously, the next step is to figure out why," replied Sumaya. "The root-cause could be anything from women sneaking birth control behind their husband's backs, to a mutual decision by the husbands and the girls to have fewer kids. Or, the men and/or girls could be less fertile due to any number of reasons…"

Jane continued paging through the research plan as Sumaya talked her through it. When they reached the end, Jane set the study in front of her on the table and smiled.

"I have to say, it seems like a pretty damn good plan, Sumaya. I see a few holes here and there, but they're all easy tweaks."

"Really?" Sumaya beamed. "That means so much coming from you, Jane, because I'd really appreciate your guidance. I've never done a *real* medical study before."

"You did research projects at university, didn't you?"

"Well, sure, but those were simple studies," responded Sumaya, "where I usually knew what the results were going to be before I started. But you have done dozens of big research projects like this."

Jane picked up the proposal and began paging through it again.

"Your outline is fantastic, but there's no way that you can do this all by yourself. You'll need lots of help, and it won't be cheap." Jane looked up and grinned, "Do you think that I'm made of money or what?"

"Oh, no, Jane." Sumaya shook her head, "I'm sorry. That wasn't what I was implying at all. I want to apply for a grant from the UN, or MSF, or the National Institute of Health. I figured that you might know how to help me navigate the process. I would never expect you to pay for it."

"You may not be expecting, but I'm offering… In fact, I'm insisting!" Jane laughed, "I think that the results of this research could be revolutionary. I would be honored to fund it, and help you any way that I can."

"I couldn't take your money, Jane!"

"Sumaya, the whole point of having money is to use it to do great things! I think that you may be on the cusp of something remarkable here! Trust me, getting grants from the UN, or any other government-related organization, is a nightmare. It takes forever. Hell, you could have your study completed and published in the time that it takes for those idiots to approve and fund a project."

"Oh Jane, thank you!" Sumaya clapped her hands in joy. "I hate to take advantage of your friendship, but I certainly do appreciate it!"

"No problem" replied Jane, as she took a red pen out of her purse and began marking up the document. "The biggest problem that I see is that you're assuming you'll be doing too many tasks yourself."

"I'm not afraid of long hours, Jane, you know that."

"Just because you have every advantageous genetic mutation known to man doesn't mean that you're Wonder Woman. The first step to success is to hire great people, and then *you* need to focus on managing *their* work."

"But I've never been a manager," replied Sumaya.

Jane scoffed, "You do a great job of managing me, and the rest of the clinic employees. You've been doing it every day for over a year now. You'll do fine."

Jane looked back down at the document and continued bleeding on it with her red pen.

"You're also going to need far more lab equipment and computers than you're accounting for. We want to get those answers as quickly as possible, so we need to order extra resources upfront. That will give us the option of quickly redirecting the research in whatever direction the data takes us. We don't want to be delayed by having to send samples back to Europe, or back to the U.S. for analysis. We need to be able to do everything right here in Sudan."

Sumaya grimaced, "That's going to cost a fortune."

"Listen, Sumaya. I know that you're young. You youngsters think that you have all the time in world. But I'm funding this thing; and, at the ripe age of forty-one, I'm pretty much an old lady. So, I want to get answers fast, and I really don't care how much money it costs me to speed things up."

CHAPTER 31

We'll Always Have Paris

"Brothers and Sisters! We've had eight overflies this week alone. We can no longer stand idly by. The outsiders are never going to leave us to ourselves. We need to shed this yoke of persecution and move on from this god-forsaken commonwealth if we ever hope to live in peace. And we must do it now!"

The barn responded with polite applause.

Most people incorrectly believe, because the Mennonites and Amish live a relatively simple lifestyle, that they are also poor. These are the same people who assume that a person driving a new leased Mercedes has enormous wealth. That Mercedes driver often owns nothing more than an enormous pile of debt.

This particular clan of Mennonites, in fact, enjoyed a trade surplus with the outside world that would have made the People's Republic of China blush. They were master craftsmen whose products sold for top dollar. The organic food fad had turned Mennonite-grown crops into an ultra-expensive urban delicacy. Since they grew their own food, made their own clothes and even milled their own lumber from the forests that they owned, piles of cash flowed into the community while virtually no cash flowed out. The Mennonites saved virtually every penny that they earned. The community kept its wealth stored in under-ground safes in the form of cash, silver and gold. Those safes, hidden under their barns, and in their root cellars, were now bursting at the seams.

Mennonite villages and sects take many forms. There is no world-wide leadership. There is no such thing as a *Mennonite pope* who dictates the rules and customs of their way of life. As a result, each community adheres to slightly different beliefs. Most refuse to use electrical power from the grid or talk on land-line telephones, but, strangely, many sects do permit off-the-grid solar panels and cell phones. The issue is more about avoiding the "danger" of a wire connecting them to the evils of the outside world verses an outright disdain for technology. Solar panels and cell phones eliminate the need for a hard wire back to civilization, so many Mennonites find them acceptable, if they are modest in their use.

The community prohibited personal laptops and iPads in private homes, fearing that they could be used to foster evil personal traits like pleasure, vanity, and envy. The community did, however, have a computer-room filled with rather ancient desk-top PCs powered by solar panels and rechargeable batteries. These older-model computers included wireless internet access, but it was strictly monitored and censored.

Brother Elijah continued his speech in front of the congregation, "There are many locations where we can be much safer than we are here in Pennsylvania. We need protection from the external-Satans who are hell-bent on destroying us with their genetic engineering aerial bombardment. Brother Caleb and I have found some superb potential locations to reconstitute our community..."

Brother Caleb approached the podium to address the gathering.

"In Osage City, in the great state of Kansas, we found a so-called Atlas E site for sale. Back in the 1960's the U.S. government paid over three million dollars to build this facility, the modern value of that price is over 30-million dollars. Today, however, it is offered for only $210,000."

The room nodded their heads in approval.

"It's in a very secluded part of Kansas. It has 15,000 sq. ft. of hardened underground floor-space and several hardened above-ground concrete structures. The facility only comes with twenty-five above-ground acres, but it is all fenced. In addition, there are over 20,000 acres of excellent farm land and forests for sale immediately surrounding the facility, most for less than one thousand dollars per acre, so, we will have plenty of room for expansion."

"Not to mention, it has a grass landing strip which our cows can use for grazing!"

The crowd laughed because, of course, Mennonites were forbidden from using airplanes, so their cows would be perfectly safe nibbling the runway for lunch.

"Thank you, brother Caleb," stated Brother Elijah as he re-approached the podium. "The other promising site that we found was just outside of the small town of Paris, in rural

Missouri. This seller is asking $245,000, but he is highly-motivated and may accept a lower offer. It comes with thirteen acres of land, and includes 11,200 square feet of nuclear-hardened, underground floor space. It has 24-inch thick concrete walls and ceilings. It has EMP shielding, blast doors, blast valves, two alternate escape hatches in addition to the main doors. It has six air vents with a filtration system, an underground fuel storage tank, lighting, sewage ejector pumps, heating, cooling, dehumidification and an electric hoist for getting things into and out of the bunker – all of which are fully functional. And all can be operated off the grid. The property is surrounded by an eight-foot-tall chain link fence, excellent water wells, and two 10,000-gallon stainless steel water storage tanks. As with the Atlas E site in Osage City, there are thousands of acres of farm land for sale surrounding the plot in Paris, all for under one thousand dollars per acre."

Caleb interjected, "The point is that, with either option, we can sell our land here for $2,000-3,000 per acre, and use those funds to triple the amount of land we can farm at the new location. We just need to be willing to move."

Sister Sarah, Jane's daughter, struggling to manage the two babies in her lap, raised her hand with a question. "What are these places? Why are they so cheap?"

"*Atlas E* was, obviously, an old atomic missile silo," Brother Caleb answered. "Due to treaties with Russia in the 1970's, the U.S. government was forced to either destroy or sell many of their nuclear weapon sites. It would have cost the government millions of dollars to crush these structures with their 24-inch-thick concrete walls. To save money, many of the silos were sold to neighboring towns for next to nothing. Sometimes for only one dollar.

Elijah continued answering Sarah's question, "The Paris, Missouri bunker is a little different. It was built by AT&T under a contract from the government. It was part of a system of underground, nuclear-hardened, telephone booster stations that were built in the 1960's to ensure uninterrupted communications in the event of a nuclear attack. These were maintained by the U.S. government through the mid 1990's. So, the Paris facility is in somewhat better shape than the Atlas E facility in Kansas."

"Which option do you recommend, Brother Elijah?" asked Sister Sarah.

"They are both perfect for our needs and very affordable. They will both protect our community and our precious children from anything the outside world decides to throw at us. The Atlas E facility is very remote which I, personally, like. There are very few towns within fifty miles of that site. However, being an older structure, it will need more work. In addition, it's 350 miles further away from our current location than the other option. The Paris site is closer and requires less restoration, but it's not as remote and there are several towns within fifty miles."

Discussions in the barn went on well into the night and continued for another ten days. Eventually the town came to a consensus that the additional 350-mile trek while carrying everything they owned in horse-drawn wagons, was not worth the additional solitude of the Atlas E site. The community of Mennonites opted for the closer and more updated facility. They purchased the bunker, sold their existing land in Pennsylvania for top dollar, and bought several hundred thousand acres of farm and forest-land in Missouri at fire-sale prices. The community loaded up their wagons and pointed their horses towards Paris.

CHAPTER 32

Seoul Women

December 15, 2048

It was a brisk Tuesday morning. Jane and Sumaya were doing some pre-run stretching on the steps outside the luxurious lobby of the Four Seasons Hotel in Seoul, South Korea. They were waiting for Jane's friend from medical school, Mi-Na Kim, who was now a senior writer for *The Lancet*, the world's premier medical journal. Jane had agreed to give Mi-na an exclusive interview prior to the presentation of her and Sumaya's highly-anticipated paper later that day. Jane always enjoyed touring unfamiliar cities by running through their streets and she looked forward to having her dear friend Mi-na, a native of Seoul, show her the town.

At 6:24 a.m. a silver sedan pulled up to the hotel's steps and Mi-na bounced out.

"Ann yeong ha se yo!" said Mi-na

"Ann yeong ha se yo!" replied Jane.

For being such an efficient country, Jane thought it was strange that Koreans required a five-word phase to say something as simple as, "hello!"

"It's great to see you again," exclaimed Jane as she galloped down the steps to hug her friend, "and you're five minutes early!"

"Please! I could have been thirty minutes early and I still wouldn't have been here before you, Ms. Punctuality."

"I have no idea what you're referring to!"

The two laughed as Jane performed the introductions. "Mi-na, this is my colleague Dr. Sumaya. Sumaya, this is my dear friend, Mi-na. We studied together at Mayo."

Mi-na shook Sumaya's hand. "It's a pleasure to meet you, Dr. Sumaya. We've heard so much about you… And so many rumors about your research and your results. I'm incredibly excited and honored that you're granting me the first interview."

Mina pulled out three small microphones and clipped them on the collars of everyone's running gear.

"I hope you don't mind if I record this," said Mi-na. "I can't take notes while we're running, and I don't want to rely on my memory and risk misquoting you."

"I don't mind at all," replied Jane. "We need to get everything correct."

Sumaya chimed in, "That's one reason why we delayed releasing our results. We wanted to ensure that our findings were 100% accurate."

"Let's put some miles behind us!" exclaimed Jane. "Mi-na, please lead the way. Show us Seoul!"

"To the Blue House!" replied Mi-na as she took off at a pace that was nearly a sprint, with Jane and Sumaya nipping at her heels.

"The Blue House is sort of like Korea's version of the White House, right?" asked Sumaya.

"Yes," replied Mi-Na, "It's a mile or so north of here. After that we'll loop back south and see some of the other sites. You've already toured the Demilitarized Zone?"

"The DMZ was so bizarre!" exclaimed Sumaya. "We went on the normal tour, but then Jane got us special access since she's such a B.A."

Jane laughed, "Please. It was no big deal. I had worked with General Bassett on a few programs in the past, so he hooked us up to play *the most dangerous hole in golf.* It was pretty cool."

The hole is on the edge of Camp Bonifas. It's a 185-yard, par 3, located right on the border with North Korea. The tee box is on the roof an abandoned machine gun nest. The green is surrounded by bunkers. Not sand trap bunkers like a normal golf course, but real armored bunkers.

"It was scary as hell!" Sumaya exclaimed. "If you miss the fairway to the left, you end up in an active mine field, and if you miss to the right, your ball rolls down into a real military trench, set up to repel the North Koreans the next time that they decide to attack the South."

"It was surreal," Jane agreed. "My legs were shaking like Jell-O. I'm surprised I even made contact with the ball."

Mi-na replied. "Camp Bonifas is named after Army Captain Arthur Bonifas. He was hacked to death by a bunch of axe-wielding North Korean troops during a disagreement over the pruning of a poplar tree. Can you believe that? Murdered over a tree! It doesn't get much crazier than that."

The three women looped around the Blue house at a blistering pace of just under six minutes per mile, and then turned back south.

"Did you hike the infiltration tunnels?"

"Yes, we did," replied Jane. "It's amazing that the North Koreans still claim that those tunnels were coal mines, and that they dug under the border by accident!"

"Right?" Mi-Na agreed. "There wasn't an ounce of coal in any of those tunnels. They were all solid granite. In some areas, you could see where the North Koreans had sprayed the granite walls with black spray paint, trying to justify their bat-crazy coal story."

Sumaya chimed in, "We walked the whole stretch of the tunnel, right up to the cement wall at the North Korean border."

As they circled back south, the trio passed Seoul City Hall. After navigating another mile or so of crowded city sidewalks, they entered the tranquility of Nansan Park. Located in the center of Seoul, the park is home to Nansan Mountain and the Seoul Tower. It can be seen from the entire city. The women ran under the cable cars carrying tourists to the *Seoul Tower* atop Nansan Mountain but the girls wouldn't be riding the lift on this trip. Instead, they scrambled up the steep, winding mountain path on foot.

"Well ladies, as much I love hearing about your exploration of my country, at the end of the day I am medical reporter, not a travel writer. So, let's get down to business. The scuttlebutt in the scientific community is that you will be presenting a ground-breaking paper at the

Global Genetic Conference this afternoon. The buzz is incredible. I've never seen such commotion over something that virtually no one has even seen."

Jane went first, "Here's the *Reader's Digest* version, Mi-Na. A year and a half ago, the two of us were working for MSF in the Sudan when Sumaya had this bright idea that she wanted to figure out why the birth rates in our village seemed to be declining after increasing for years."

The three were breathing heavy as they ran up the steep trail and approached the iconic Seoul Tower, situated on the peak of Nansan Mountain.

Jane continued, "In the end, Sumaya's idea for a simple study turned into, what may be, a world-altering scientific discovery. The paper we are presenting documents what we found."

"But why all the secrecy? Why didn't you release some interim reports with preliminary results?"

"It's not that simple," stated Sumaya. "Like I pointed out earlier, we wanted to make sure that all our findings were correct. We didn't want to risk putting the world into a wild-ass frenzy over either bad data, or misguided interpretations of good data."

"Well, you've certainly succeeded in getting everyone riled up now. So, it's time to spill the beans, ladies. What did you find?"

"First, we did confirm that the birth rates in Terekeka were actually dropping, and they continue to drop. We established that it was *not* due to socio-economic reasons or couples deciding to have fewer kids. The problem is physical infertility, and the phenomenon is widespread. It's not limited to Terekeka."

"So, is it some sort of widespread genetic plumbing problem?" asked Mi-Na. "Blocked fallopian tubes or some such thing?"

"Unfortunately, no," Sumaya grimaced. "A plumbing problem could be fixed with surgery or even in-vitro fertilization. This is an egg and sperm problem."

The trio paused at the top of Nansan Mountain and briefly soaked in the 360-degree panoramic view of the sprawling, affluent, mega-city of Seoul. Twenty-six million people in the metropolitan area, all within howitzer-shell range of North Korea. Sumaya and Jane snapped a few pictures of the view from the peak. They could clearly see the Han River cutting through the center of the city. Beyond the Han, off in the haze, they could see the ritzy Gangnam section of Seoul. Known as the Beverley Hills of Korea, it was made famous by Psy Park Jae-sang when he recorded his 2012 hit, *Gangnam Style*. The girls then then sprinted back down the mountain and looped back north once again.

Sumaya continued, "As you know, the nucleus of an unfertilized human egg, or any unfertilized egg for that matter, contains the mother's genetic material, her chromosomes, which contain her genes. Unfertilized eggs and sperms only contain half as many chromosomes as a normal cell."

Mi-Na interjected, "Yes, twenty-three individual chromosomes vs the normal forty-six chromosomes which are made up of twenty-three pairs."

"Correct," replied Sumaya. "So, when the sperm combines with the egg, the result is a full set of 46 individual chromosomes, 23 pairs. The egg starts dividing and bada-bing, bada-boom – you have the miracle of life."

Mi-na was anxious to get to the point. "Yes, that's how babies are made. So, what's the problem in Terekeka?"

Jane chuckled, "Well, Terekeka has plenty of problems, but the problem that we are talking about here relates to the zona pellucida and the plasma membrane."

Mi-na jumped in, "OK. The zona pellucida is the egg-wall that holds in the cytoplasm. When the egg is mature, the zona pellucida has a special feature that allows the sperm to infiltrate and fertilize the egg."

"Correct," Jane responded. "Fertilization is *not* this macho process where a bunch of sperm swim full speed towards an egg and one of them finally hits it hard enough to break through and win the prize. It's more complicated and subtle than that. It's more like the sperm snuggles up to the wall of the egg, and then fuses with the outer layers of the egg wall."

"Ha! Snuggle!" Mi-Na laughed. "Interesting word choice when referring to sperm."

Sumaya continued the explanation, "Once the sperm snuggles up to the egg wall, the acrosome, which is the cap-like thing on a sperm's head, goes to work. The entire sperm is also covered by a plasma membrane, sort of like a skin. When the sperm attaches to the egg, the plasma membrane on the sperm's head opens and the contents of the sperm's acrosome starts working on the egg's zona pellucida. As you know, this is called the acrosome reaction. The sperm releases two enzymes, hyaluronidase and acrosin that eventually digest a hole in the egg's zona pellucida, allowing the sperm to enter."

Mi-Na nodded, "And then, the zona pellucida releases a calcium influx, which causes a signaling cascade, which prevents additional sperm from binding to the egg."

The trio were now racing past the Gyeongbokgung Royal Palace. Built in the fifteenth century, it was a spectacular complex of palaces, gardens and shrines, but they didn't take much notice. Their focus was now centered around the topic at hand and maintaining their blistering pace.

"OK, so you've broken down how the process of making babies is supposed to work. Where are things going wrong?"

"We discovered that around half of the twelve and thirteen-year-old child brides in Terekeka now appear to be sterile. The problem is that their zona pellucidas are rock hard, and can't be infiltrated by the sperm for fertilization. It's a well-known fact that egg-walls harden with age which, is one reason why most older women can't get pregnant. But in this case, these pre-teen girls have eggs as hard as those of a 75-year-old woman."

"But isn't that treatable?" asked Mi-Na. "I've seen similar cases where LASERs or special chemicals were used to open a hole in the egg for the sperm to enter. I think that they call it 'assist in hatching'?"

"Yes," answered Jane. "We've attempted all known methods of softening these hardened zona pellucida, but none of them have worked. And the sperm's penetration of the egg isn't the only problem. These egg shells are so hard that they also prevent the clusters of splitting cells from breaking out of the zona pellucida even if it is fertilized. The rock-hard shell crushes and kills the cells inside the egg when they split and try to expand."

"Well, that doesn't sound promising," Mi-Na sighed, "You said there was a sperm problem too?"

"The sperm issue mirrors the egg problem. The skin of the sperm hardens, just like the zona pellucida, and this creates two problems," Sumaya explained. "First, when the plasma membrane gets too hard, the sperm's tail becomes less flexible and it can't swim as fast. The second problem is that the plasma membrane covers the acrosome on the head of the sperm. When that membrane gets too hard, it prevents the acrosome from being released when a sperm encounters the egg."

"What do you guys think is causing it?" Mi-Na asked. "A virus? Bacteria? Something in the water or food supply?"

Jane shook her head, "Nope. We ruled out all of those possible causes, and at least a dozen others."

"So, what is the cause?"

Jane and Sumaya both glanced at each other and hesitated as they continued running.

Finally, Jane spoke up, "We think that it is caused by the gene-mutation enhancements that that were given to the ancestors of these girls and young men thirty years ago."

"Woah, woah, hold on a second," Mi-na yelled, bringing their run to a halt. "*That's* the hypothesis of your paper? What the hell are you doing, Jane? Sumaya's young. You, on the other hand, have been around the block and back again. You should know better than this."

"Mi-na, our methodology and the resulting data is concrete. We've covered all the bases, and then we went back and covered them all two or three more times."

"Give me a break! Those bases were all covered years ago, Jane. It was scientifically proven through multiple studies that those *Big Five* gene-mutation enhancement therapies were both safe and effective. And not only for the people who received them. We showed that those enhancements were totally safe for their off-spring as well! You two will be thrown into the same bucket as the conspiracy theorists who think that childhood vaccinations cause autism or that we faked the moon landings!"

"No. There's a huge difference between conspiracy theories and what we are claiming. We have facts," insisted Jane. "Yes, the data from GammaTek showed that those who underwent gene-mutation enhancement, and even the first generation of their offspring, had no reproduction problems, and that birthrates even improved, but that's where their data stops. Our new data starts at the point where their studies were halted."

"Our paper not only explains exactly *what* is happening, it also describes *why* it is happening," Sumaya stated with an air of confidence.

Mi-na rolled her eyes and sighed, "Fine, ladies. Enlighten me!"

"The reason that we started seeing the problem in Terekeka before anywhere else in the world is due to the unique combination of Terekeka being an early adopter of gene therapy, and their atrocious cultural norm of getting pre-teens pregnant."

Sumaya jumped in, "We measured a steady increase in the hardness of the zona pellucidas, and the plasma membrane of the sperm, from one generation to the next. In the first generation, this slight hardening actually makes the egg and sperm perform slightly better, which does increase fertility, hence the boom. But then, generation after generation, *something* in that gene-mutation enhancement cocktail causes this ever-increasing hardening issue. By the third generation after the Big Five treatment, around 80% of both men and women are essentially sterile. We predict that by the fourth generation 98% will be sterile, and by the fifth generation all will be sterile."

Jane nodded, "The scariest part is that the *Big Five* cocktail includes a gene-drive function, with a power of well over 90%. So, unfortunately, nothing can stop it."

The information now started making sense to Mi-Na. "So, what you are saying is that if anyone who does *not* have the mutation mates with someone who *has* the mutation, their offspring will almost always have the mutation?"

Sumaya continued. "Yes. That's the glory, or the curse, of gene-drive. Within a few generations, the gene drive feature is going to spread the *Big Five* gene-mutation enhancement to virtually everyone on the planet…"

Mi-na's face sobered, she finally understood full gravity of the problem. "I suppose that does make sense. That's exactly why the gene-drive feature was added to the treatment in the first place -- to ensure, in the interest of fairness, that all future generations would receive the *Big Five* enhancements through conception."

"The fertility issue is only showing up in a few places right now because not many *Big Five* third generation kids have been born yet, much less made it to the age of reproduction. But the progression of this infertility problem in the human race is now virtually unstoppable."

"No," Mi-na shook her head in disbelief. "That can't be. With all our genetic advancements, there has to be something that can be done to reverse this."

Sumaya shrugged her shoulders. "Not that we've seen. That's part of what took us so long to publish. We didn't want to put a problem on the table without also offering a solution. We've tried dozens of strategies to reverse this. Unfortunately, even with the latest CRISPR technologies we've been painfully unsuccessful."

"Gene-drive is a powerful trait," Jane added, "We've used CRISPR to create several counter-treatments which unwound some of the Big Five gene modifications temporarily. Unfortunately, the gene-drive trait kept flipping our changes back. Once we release our findings, then, maybe someone else will be able to create a fix, but we're not too optimistic."

Mi-Na stared at the two women in total silence. After thirty seconds, she glanced up at the sky, "I have never been a big believer in a God, but if there is one, then God help us."

CHAPTER 33

The Presentation

December 16, 2048

Sumaya was more nervous than she had ever been in her entire life. Her presentation had been moved from a standard conference room, to the *Four Seasons'* massive grand ballroom. The venue was packed. It was standing room only. Conference attendees were stacked along the walls like cord wood. The Seoul fire marshal would have been less than pleased. Hundreds of scientists were blocking every isle in the room.

The crowd was polite and listened attentively to Sumaya's overview of their paper and their findings. When Jane joined her colleague at the podium for questions-and-answers, however, all hell broke loose. The comments from the floor were less than supportive, to put it mildly.

"It is totally irresponsible and unprecedented to present an un-peer-reviewed paper like this. It is beneath dignity of this conference!"

"It's reckless to publicize a theory which is so controversial, before it has even undergone a peer-review."

"Why did the committee even allow this paper to be presented?"

Jane responded calmly and tried to maintain her composure. "All of the conclusions in this paper are thoroughly backed by hard data which has been checked, double, and triple-checked."."

"This is crazy! Why wasn't there an open and transparent peer-review!" one scientist shouted.

Jane sighed, "Here's the problem: The data, and the conclusions that were drawn from the data, are so incendiary that we couldn't allow an open peer-review. Not until we were confident that it was all correct. But now you *all* have access to *all* of our data. You are more than welcome to peer-review the crap out of our findings until the cows come home!"

"Jane, you know damn well that's not the way things are supposed to be done!" another scientist criticized.

"If we were talking about normal science in normal times I would totally agree with you, unfortunately, nothing about this situation is normal."

Jane pointed to a reporter in the third row for the next question.

"Hello. I'm Alison Austin, Science editor for the Boston Harrold. I admit that I didn't follow every detail that you presented, but, to me, it almost sounded -- like your conclusion was that -- this might lead to the end of human civilization as we know it?"

There was a long silence. Jane then leaned into the microphone and uttered a single word, "Yes."

Mayhem erupted. Everyone was yelling. Audience members were arguing with the person next to them one moment, and screaming at the person behind them the next. Half of the PhDs in the room agreed that a genetic apocalypse could be at hand. The other half thought that Jane and Sumaya were nuts, or that their data was flawed, or that their conclusions were overblown.

The session chairman approached the podium, muscling his way between Jane and Sumaya. He grabbed the microphone, and tried in vain to bring the packed ballroom to order. All Jane and Sumaya could do was look at each other and shake their heads.

As the PhD's in the room continued screaming at each other, Jane noticed that the reporters in the room were running for the exits. They were in a mad dash to file their bi-lines for a story that could be, not just the story of the century, but the most important story in the history of mankind.

CHAPTER 34

A Decade Later

December 31, 2056

It was New Year's Eve, nearly nine years after the release of their landmark paper. Jane and Sumaya were in New York City, hovering above Times Square, sitting in the seventh-floor restaurant of New York's Marriot Marque. Their table was ideally situated next to a floor-to-ceiling curved window hanging out over the center of Times Square. The street below them, Broadway between 45th and 46th Street, was filled with frozen masses of humanity, waiting for the famous ball to drop.

"It's so great to catch up with you, Jane."

"Far too long, my friend!" Jane smiled.

"I can't believe that you, of all people, are moving to a Mennonite community?"

"Yes. Unfortunately, this will be one of my last nights of drinking," sighed Jane as she took a large chug of Dom Perignon. "On the bright side, I am betrothed to a wonderful man. He's Sarah's husband's uncle. His name is Joseph."

Sumaya raised her eyebrows, "Wow, really?"

"Yep! With all my free time, lately, I've had more opportunity to visit with Sarah and my grandkids, which increased my urge to be closer to them. And then, one evening, I was introduced to Joseph at a big extended family dinner. His wife passed away two years ago from breast cancer. He was ready to move on. And it all just sort of fell into place. Strange where life's meandering path will lead you."

"Well, congratulations," Sumaya said as they toasted their champagne flutes.

Jane laughed, "So, could you please stop setting me up with every middle-aged guy you find at conferences… or in grocery stores?"

"I guess that I need to find a new hobby."

Over the past decade, the duo had become internationally known for their world-changing discovery. In some circles, they were hailed as heroes. But in others, they were trolled as pariahs. Often, people treated them as if they had created the problem, when all they had done was uncover it. Many looked to Jane and Sumaya for a solution. The pair had been asked to serve on countless boards and had co-chaired several high-profile UN committees on the topic. But, at least for Jane, the pressure and publicity had gotten old.

Sumaya was certain that Jane's desire to get away from the stress was behind her sudden desire to abandon the modern world for life as a Mennonite wife.

"Well, Sumaya, it took almost a decade, but finally *almost* everyone agrees that you and I were correct.

"It's a shame that governments were so slow to see the light. Even five years after our paper was published, some countries were still imposing the genetic enhancement cocktails on their few remaining non-mutated children. All in the name of giving their country a strategic advantage."

From their toasty warm seats in the luxury restaurant, far above the street, Jane and Sumaya people-watched the shivering masses huddled seven stories below them. The crowd didn't seem nearly as festive as previous years. On the other hand, no one seemed too festive about much of anything anymore. A nagging lack of optimism in the future showed itself in many ways. All over the world, stock markets were trapped in a never-ending downward spiral. Real estate prices plunged. Global investment had tanked. Even technical innovation ground to a halt. The universal mindset was: Why try to accomplish great things? Why invest in a better future, if there isn't going to be a future?

"Hey, maybe you and your new Mennonite hubby can crank out some non-mutant children to help keep civilization going!" Sumaya joked.

Jane laughed, "The world may be desperate for non-mutated babies, but I don't think it's quite *that* desperate. No one needs me attempting to reproduce at 50."

Enough time had passed that the third generation of gene enhancement ancestors were now coming of age all over the world. This was causing a very measurable decline in the entire planet's birth rate. Of course, not everyone was on their third generation. Some couples were only second-generation mutations, and they were still having children, which was why birth rates were nowhere near zero. Those second-generation couples, however, were now fully aware that they would never have grand-children, that their third-generation children were doomed to sterility.

Meanwhile, the United Nations had executed an ambitious program to genetically-test the world's entire population. It was supposed to be a global genetic census to determine the numbers and ages of all first, second and third generation mutations. The most important objective, however, was to identify those few remaining humans who were unaffected. That group was now referred to as non-mutants, or NoMs. Even though participation in the UN genetic-census program was supposed to be mandatory, the actual participation-rate had only been around 60%, because the public's trust in government organizations had plunged to an all-time low.

Jane and Sumaya may have been celebrating the dawn of a New Year that evening, but, true to form, they couldn't stop working. Both had brought copies of a recently released UN report, which they reviewed sporadically between drinks and conversation.

Of the seven billion people on the Earth:

4,938,436,324 had agreed to be tested.

4,937,943,609 of those tested were found to be mutated

532,715 were not mutated

However, of those who were not mutated, the overwhelming majority were too old to reliably reproduce:

378,973 were over 70

111,870 were between 50 and 70

37,290 were between 40 and 50

4,262 were between 18 and 40

320 were under 18

Jane laid her copy of the report on the table, and ordered another drink. "So, according to these statistics, there are fewer than 5,000 people under the age of forty, who still *might* be able to produce non-mutant offspring. Can we really rebuild society with such a tiny viable population?"

"It is definitely possible. 195,000 years ago, during one of the Earth's deadly global-cooling periods, and then again, 70,000 years ago, after the Sumatra/Toba super-eruption, the number of humans, grand-total, world-wide, was reduced to a breeding population of only around 1,000 people. And even back then, as ignorant cave-people, humanity recovered from both of those disasters just fine", replied Sumaya. "The problem we have today is that, most of those 4,262 NoMs in the 18-40 age-group, over 3,000 of them, are already married, or they are in a committed relationship with partners who *have* mutations."

Jane sighed, "I guess that makes sense. With four billion people surveyed, and only 4,000 non-mutations of child-bearing age, the chances of any one of those non-mutations shacking up with another NoM is roughly one in a million. It's highly unlikely that any two of those young NoMs would happen to hook up by chance."

"There *are* options. The UN could pay non-mutants to ditch their genetically-doomed significant-others and pair up with other non-mutants. Or they could pay NoM women to be artificially inseminated with sperm from non-mutant males."

Jane was frustrated. "I get that both situations are highly unromantic, but I don't see why people can't just suck it up and take one for the team -- for the future of humanity!" Jane then paused for a moment. "On the other hand, I'm marrying a man I barely know and joining a Mennonite community. So, maybe I have no business judging other people's love lives."

Sumaya laughed, then continued analyzing the report. "It looks like there are 320 NoMs who are eighteen and under."

"I'd say that they are our best hope for the long term. Did the report break down exactly how old they all are?" Jane asked.

"Most are in the fifteen to eighteen range," answered Sumaya. "The problem is that it isn't a diverse gene pool at all. Those 320 kids come from fifty-eight sets of parents, and many have at least one great-grand-parent in common."

"So, if they reproduced, we could end up with an entirely new set of turds in our limited gene-pool, due to inbreeding?"

"Yep, and then there are the cultural issues. With such a wide variety of religions and ethnicities amongst the non-mutants, those who want to reproduce with 'their own kind' are almost guaranteed to run into incest issues down the line."

Sumaya groaned and slapped her report on the table in frustration. "It's all such a mess! Society is unraveling. Chaos is king. How do you convince someone to abandon their way-of-life to reproduce with a total stranger, solely for the sake of the Earth's genetic diversity? Who would make that kind of sacrifice just to save such a screwed-up world?"

"I don't know." sighed Jane, staring out the window as the shimmering crystal-covered ball started to drop. "All I know is that, for the future of mankind, it *has* to happen."

Fireworks and confetti consumed the sky as the frozen hoards standing in the streets below them cheered in unison.

The hope of a New Year was in the air, but so too was a healthy dose fear and dread.

One week later, Jane and Sumaya were in Manhattan's Turtle Bay neighborhood, standing in the office of Oyvind Knudsen, the Secretary General of the United Nations. Oyvind's massive, luxuriously appointed office filled most of the 39th floor of the UN headquarters' building. Jane and Sumaya had been invited to brief the Secretary General and his staff. In a little over fifteen minutes, the pair concisely explained the scope of the problem, the potential solutions, and the pros and cons of the various solutions. Jane wrapped up the presentation by making it clear that no matter which route was chosen, the most difficult part would be convincing the non-mutants to participate.

Secretary Knudsen had turned his back on the women as he wandered across his office and pulled back the curtains covering an oversized window. He gazed through the snow flurries at the chunks of ice floating in the East River far below.

"Ladies, I'm certainly not worried about pandering to these damn NoM's feelings. Just tell me which option you feel is the best. I will see to it that the NoMs comply. Of this, I can assure you!"

CHAPTER 35

The Island of NoMs

The warm Caribbean sea-breeze repeatedly disheveled Oyvind Knudsen's normally well-kept Scandinavian hair. The Secretary General of the United Nations and his German deputy, Morgan Paul, were standing next to the luxurious rooftop pool, atop the island's thirty-five-story main housing structure. The island of Bimini, in the Bahamas, had never looked better. Over the past eight years, the UN had purchased the entire island from the Bahamas, and then radically transformed it. The previously laid-back oasis was now covered with brand new parks, recreational facilities, bars, museums, golf courses, and a harbor filled with every type of boat imaginable. The _Bimini Project_ was the ultimate UN experiment. It was designed to be a genetic Noah's Ark, specifically created to rescue humanity from annihilation.

The original approvals for the *Bimini Project* had gone surprisingly well. To the surprise of all, there had been virtually no push-back from Russia.

The Russians were notorious for their long-standing nationalistic history – firmly believing that they were superior to all other countries. Russia also had a long history of using performance-enhancing drugs, both on their world-class athletes, and within their military services. When CRISPR was invented, genetic labs immediately sprang up all over Russia. Those labs quickly became the largest consumers of CRISPR kits, and eventually, the largest producers of CRISPR kits on the planet. Their lack of regulations resulted in Russia becoming a hotbed of often crazy human genetic experimentation. Many of those experiments were disastrous. But they learned from their failures, and, in the end, the Russians led the world in many areas of genetic manipulation.

Due to their insatiable desire for national superiority, Russia was the first country in the world to mandate a regimen of genetic treatments for all of its citizens. CRISPR-based modifications were added to Russia's standard set of vaccinations for all of its infants and children. This meant that Russia now had zero NoM citizens who qualified for the UN's Bimini Project. Because of this, the Security Council was certain that the Russians would vehemently object to, and ultimately veto, the *Bimini Project*. To everyone's surprise, the Russians did not exercise their veto, and the program moved forward.

The *Bimini Project* was expensive. The UN paid for every square inch of the island at least four times over: First, the UN purchased the island from the nation of the

Bahamas. Second, they had to pay each of the island's residents to leave their homes and move to another island. For this, the UN paid at least double the previous market-price of each home and business, plus moving expenses. Then the UN had to pay to tear down virtually every existing structure on the island. Then the entire island was rebuilt and transformed into the gleaming oasis that Secretary Knudsen had envisioned. Finally, the UN had to pay each NoM a king's ransom to leave their homes, leave their families, and move to the island. Once there, their "job" was to meet and mate with other NoMs, all of whom were presently total strangers.

"It certainly is a beautiful sight," commented Deputy Secretary Morgan Paul, as he and his boss surveyed the glorious resort.

Oyvind scoffed, "It sucks that it took us four years longer than planned to build this monstrosity. And it *really* burns me up that it's over-budget by a factor of three. But you're right, it *is* beautiful."

"I saw a poll this morning indicating that both mutations and NoMs are now overwhelmingly opposed to it".

"Of course they are! Everyone hates it! I hate it! It's a horrible solution. But out of all the horrible solutions we had to choose from, this was the *least* horrible option in the bunch. What was the final count of NoMs who agreed to move?"

"1,183"

Oyvind sighed. "Not nearly as many as we had hoped for, but it's a hell of a lot better than where we started."

Originally, the UN had offered NoMs a $500,000 bonus to relocate. In addition to this one-time bonus, they were offered free room and board on Bimini for life, or for as long as they remained on the island. The response to this offer was underwhelming to put it mildly. Only 287 NoMs had agreed to participate. The UN eventually increased the offer to $16 million per person, amortized over ten years, after which they could leave the island if they wished.

Participation was still far less than 100% due to the fact many of the twenty to thirty-something NoMs were already married to mutated spouses and had mutated children, neither of which would be allowed on the island. The cash incentive, however, was enough to convince over one-thousand NoMs to abandon their old lives to start new ones in Bimini. And, just maybe, they could save humanity in the process.

CHAPTER 36

The NoMs Arrive

Sally, a 32-year-old Norwegian NoM, gazed out the window of the Gulfstream VIII as it approached the Island of Bimini. It would be her home for the next ten years, maybe forever.

Two weeks ago, after months of discussion, she, and her mutant-husband, Oskar, had decided to file for divorce after twelve years of marriage, so that she could join the Bimini Project. A lawyer helped them split the $16-million in future payments from the UN. Half of those funds would be diverted into a trust-fund for their three children. All of their lives would now be financially comfortable, even if they would never see each other again.

Tears streamed down Sally's face. She hadn't even arrived at the island and, already, she was missing her family immensely. Was she doing right thing? Sally loved her three beautiful children -- ages six, eight and ten -- with every fiber of her being. But, even though she was a NoM, all three of her offspring had inherited _the Big Five_ mutations from her now-ex-husband, so they were not welcome on the island. Sally's family, like most on the planet, had been teetering on the verge of financial ruin for years. Both Sally and Oskar had been working between 50 and 60 hours per week, merely to keep their heads above water. There was no spare time to spend together, no chance to do anything as a family. The only time that Sally saw her kids was after they were already asleep in their beds. "This is for the best," Sally kept repeating to herself. "It's the best option for all of us."

Vicky, an English NoM, was sitting in the seat next to Sally. They had chatted briefly earlier in the flight. Vicky now saw Sally crying and tried to comfort her. "It's going to be OK. Actually, it's going to be great! This is a new beginning. Let's just make the best of it!"

Sally looked around the charter jet, filled with twenty-five strangers from across Europe, and she started crying even harder. "I don't think so, Vicky. I just learned last week that I will be the only Norwegian on the whole damn island. No one else on Bimini is going to speak my native language. To make matters worse, over half of the people on the island don't even speak my second language, English! What have I gotten myself into?"

Vicky patted Sally on the arm. "Those hacks from the UN must have dreamed-up a solution for the language and cultural barriers. Stop worrying about all of the 'what ifs' and just try to make the best of it."

There was a loud thump. The reverse-thrusters roared and the tires squealed as they touched down in Bimini.

CHAPTER 37

Life in Bimini

January 9, 2065

Starting a new life is never easy, not even in paradise. But the deal that the UN made with the NoMs was pretty awesome. For the first six months, none of the NoMs on the island would be required to do *any* work. Every day was to be filled with non-stop parties and social events. The goal was to get this disparate group of people to socialize, pair up, and start reproducing as quickly as possible. Many of the new-arrivals were no longer spring chickens, and their biological clocks were ticking.

Of course, an island paradise can't function if everyone parties all the time. Even paradise needs people to trim the palm trees, pick up the trash on the beach, pour the fruity alcoholic drinks, and provide the entertainment. The UN's grand-plan was that all the work on the island, at least for the first six months, would be performed by highly-screened mutants. These workers would be shipped to Bimini every morning at the crack of dawn, and returned to a neighboring island as soon as their shifts ended. The goal was to avoid any less-than--professional interactions between the mutant workers and the NoM guests. The UN hoped that once the NoMs grew comfortable with their fellow patrons and surroundings, they would naturally take over the occupations and daily labors of the island, eliminating the need for mutant workers.

Three months into the experiment, the majority of Sally's initial reservations regarding life on Bimini had drifted away like a tropical breeze. She was adjusting quite well to her new, non-Nordic lifestyle. On one lazy Tuesday afternoon Sally was sitting at the resort's beach bar, watching the waves lap at the gorgeous pink sand, when her friend Vicky snuck up behind her.

"Sally! How are things going, darling?" Vicky gave Sally quick hug and plopped down on the barstool next to her.

"Well, Vicky, I'm consuming free drinks on a beautiful beach, at the crack of noon. Which is exactly what I did yesterday, and the day before that. So, I guess I can't complain."

The bartender served Vicky her "usual", a frozen margarita, extra Tequila, just a bit of salt on the rim, topped with a dash of OJ hand-squeezed from half an orange. The two women clinked their glasses, toasting another day in paradise.

"I agree. I'm not sure if this could ever get old!" Vicky exclaimed as she took a big gulp of her cocktail. "By the way, I saw you dancing with Ricky last night. You two seem to be hitting it off!"

"Yeah. He's okay I guess," Sally said, her tone now clearly not as chipper.

"What's wrong?" asked Vicky.

"Oh, nothing. I just video chatted with my kids and my ex this morning."

"Oh," Vicky responded, fully understanding how hard those family calls could be. "How are they doing?"

"Well, they seem to be doing great, actually. The kids love their new private school. They are playing on club teams, doing all sorts of activities. They even went on a vacation to Hawaii -- things that we never could have afforded to give them before I agreed to leave. Now that Oskar doesn't have to work as much, he gets to attend all their activities and spends far more time with them, which is awesome, because that's the whole reason we decided that I should come here, right?" Sally sighed, "I guess that I'm happy, especially because they're happy. But I must admit, I am *extremely* jealous that Oskar now gets to be a huge part of our children's lives, and I only get to talk to them for ninety minutes a month."

"Yeah, that ninety-minute communications limit really sucks. I always use up my minutes in the first week, and then it's famine for the rest of the month."

"I guess it needs to be that way. If they gave us unlimited calls, half of the island would be locked-up in their rooms talking to their former families 24-7."

"I know one thing that I'd like to keep locked-up in my room 24-7!" Vicky exclaimed flirtatiously as she eyed the tall, dark and handsome bartender who was bending over, shoveling ice into a bucket. "This new bar-boy is even hotter than the last one!"

Sally grinned, "Well of course he's hot. He's got more genetic mutations than a test-rat in a CRISPR factory."

CHAPTER 38

Mutant Life Outside of Bimini

September 21, 2065

Oyvind Knudsen, the Secretary General of the United Nations, fumed as he read the words on his laptop. In enormous 32-point font, the headline screamed *Bimini is a Failure*. The *New York Times* on-line article claimed that, after one year of operation, not only was the *Bimini Project* massively over budget, but it was achieving virtually none of its goals.

Morgan Paul, Oyvind's Chief of staff, strolled into his boss' office for the morning briefing.

"Those ungrateful, ignorant assholes!" mumbled Oyvind under his breath.

"The NoMs on Bimini?" asked Morgan.

"Yes, them too. Presently, however, I'm referring to the rest of the morons on this doomed, god-forsaken planet. Especially those hacks at *The Times*. They have no idea how hard this problem is to solve. These aren't mice in a lab, these are people's lives that we are trying to control. Sure, I'm pissed at the behavior of the damn NoMs, just like everyone else. But I'm even more pissed at those mutant staffers whom we paid good money, double what they had ever made in their lives, to work on that island."

Six months prior, there appeared to be both good and bad news coming from Bimini. The *bad* news was that there had only been six weddings thus far. The UN's master-schedule had planned for more like 40 or 50 weddings by that time. In hindsight, the expectation that complete strangers would fall in love and marry each other by the dozens, only six months after being introduced, may have been a bit aggressive.

But the *good* news had been that -- thanks partially to the fact that they were all hopped-up on fertility enhancing medications -- seventy-two of the 512 women on the island had become pregnant. Even though most of those pregnancies were out of wedlock, it meant that new NoM babies were now, finally, 'in oven', so to speak. So, the Bimini Project *appeared* to be working.

Now, however, it was six months later, one year into the project, and things weren't looking nearly as promising. The island's doctors were shocked to find that virtually all the babies who had been born in Bimini to NoM mothers, had the Big Five mutations. Genetic testing eventually determined that about one third of these mutant babies were linked to ex-spouses or boyfriends -- a result of farewell-sex just prior to leaving for Bimini. The other two-thirds of the pregnancies, however, were due to the island's hired help having illicit sex with NoM women on the island.

The UN, including the Secretary General, had known about this problem for months. The UN had tried to keep the issue under wraps, hoping that the numbers would eventually improve, but somehow the *Times* had gotten their hands on this secret information and published it. Out of the forty-five babies who had been born, only four were NoMs. One hundred and ten women were presently pregnant, most refused to undergo genetic testing of their fetuses. Out of the twenty-two women who allowed testing, all their fetuses were found to have the Big Five mutation.

"We really should have seen this coming" sighed Morgan. "I mean, this is exactly how we got into this situation in the first place, right? Why would any woman want to mate with an ugly, weak, normal NoM man when they could have themselves an attractive, brilliant, muscular mutant?"

"Those ingrate NoM women must mate with NoM men because that's what they agreed to do!" Knudsen screamed. "That's the reason that we put them on this beautiful island and made them millionaires!"

The UN Secretary threw his laptop across the room. It shattered against the wall and the pieces scattered across the office floor.

"Damn it! All they have to do is knock each other up! Is that so hard? Not only do we only have a handful of NoM babies to show for our billions in investments, to make matters worse, a good portion of our fertile NoM females are pregnant with mutated babies. So, they are all out of commission until they pop those kids out!"

The Secretary General lit a cigar and began huffing on it like a COPD patient sucking from an oxygen tank. Meanwhile, Oyvind's deputy, Morgan, meandered across the room to clean up the pieces of his boss' crumpled laptop.

CHAPTER 39

The World Begins to Rebel

September 22, 2065

At *Keat's Sports Bar*, in the Turtle Bay neighborhood of Manhattan, literally in the shadow of the UN building, Mark Austin and Kirby Kueber were munching on some pub-grub, having a conversation similar to those occurring in bars and living rooms all over the planet.

"It's un-freakiin-believable," Mark yelled as he scanned the NY Times headlines scrolling across the bottom of the bar's holographic video screens. "Over one hundred billion dollars totally wasted on those ugly-ass, good-for-nothing NoMs."

"One hundred billion of *my* hard-earned tax dollars. I am so sick of supporting those lazy, entitled pieces of crap. They get to lay around on the beach all day, drinking their fancy drinks, while we wait on them hand and foot, as if they're better than us. I say we should cut them off right now and let them rot."

Kirby took another gulp of his beer and continued ranting. "My life sucks enough as it is. We shouldn't have to support a bunch of worthless NoMs on our way to extinction."

"I heard that the Feds don't want us to refer to them as NoMs anymore. Apparently, it's considered a *genetic slur*." Mark observed in disgust.

Kirby shook his head. "How much worse can it get? For the first time since the Black Plague, Earth's human population is actually declining. And not just by a little. It's plummeting."

"Economic activity is crashing, the annual GDP of every country on Earth is declining year after year."

"And populations will continue shrinking. Huge swaths of previously populated land are turning into empty wastelands. What sort of idiot would invest in land today? It's obvious to anyone with half a brain that, with a steadily shrinking population, land is going to be worth far less ten years from now than it is today."

Mark grabbed another Coors and continued. "It's simple. Fewer people means lower demand for food, even while, new farming techniques and higher levels of carbon dioxide in the air are going to double the amount of food that can be produced per acre."

"Massive increases in food supply, coupled with decreasing demand means that previously valuable farmland will be abandoned. Wealth will evaporate. Poverty is only going to get worse. The whole situation is an unfixable mess!"

The waitress sauntered by their table. "Nurse, get us another round!" Mark demanded.

"Make that a double!"

CHAPTER 40

The Shunning

October 2, 2065

Jane and her husband, Joseph, had been feuding with the elders of the Mennonite congregation in Paris, Missouri for years. It had started almost from the day that Jane arrived in the community. There wasn't any single huge problem, it was just a long series of small disagreements which had accumulated over time. A few of their qualms were biblical, while others were related to how the Mennonite community was being managed.

Jane and Joseph were both extremely productive, and very successful. At times, this also caused resentment within the community. As time wore on, Jane and her husband unintentionally, but steadily, made adversaries of virtually everyone in the congregation. Even Jane's grandchildren, most of whom were now in their teens and twenties, no longer associated with Jane and Joseph, unless it was absolutely necessary.

Three of the community's senior Mennonite elders had requested a private meeting with Jane and Joseph. The elders hadn't disclosed the purpose of the summit, but the Jane and Joseph were fairly certain that they knew the subject of the proposed get-together.

On the day of the meeting, the elders were welcomed into Jane and Joseph's home. After a few awkward, forced pleasantries, the elders got right to the point.

"Brother Joseph, Sister Jane, we fear that your presence in our community is no longer prudent nor helpful to any of us. Sarah, we didn't want to take any actions while your grandchildren were still young. Most of them, however, are now adults or nearly adults, so there is no longer any reason to postpone the inevitable. We and the rest of the congregation's elders have unanimously voted to shun you from the community, and...."

Joseph interrupted. "Jane and I have done more for this community than any other couple, by far. Paris wouldn't be half of what it is today if it wasn't for our contributions."

"Your clear lack of humility is one of several reasons why you are being shunned Brother Joseph," Uri scolded.

"We have plenty of humility," Joseph countered. "We have worked harder than anyone to turn this facility into an impenetrable, secure fortress against the outside world. The community's coffers are overflowing. Much of that is directly due to our efforts."

"Please calm yourself, Brother Joseph. We are prepared to buy you out at a fair price, in return for your shunning,"

"Oh, isn't that so kind of you!" Joseph replied sarcastically.

The elder ignored Joseph's snide remark and continued, "However, you must agree to never return. Our offer is $250,000 for your farmhouse and land and another $200,000 for your contributions to the community. That is, $450,00 total."

Joseph looked over at Jane as she spoke for the first time. "Bring the total up to $600,000, all in gold coins, and we will leave without incident."

The elders excused themselves and huddled in a far corner of the room where they whispered for thirty seconds, and then re-emerged. "$550,000 is our final offer. Half in gold coins, and half in cash. Our last condition is that you will be required to leave before noon tomorrow."

"Deal." Joseph stood and extended his hand to the elders.

Jane still had over one hundred of million in savings and other assets outside the community. These monetary negotiations with the elders were purely a matter of principle, not of necessity.

As soon as the elders left, Joseph and Jane logged in to their unapproved personal laptops, which represented one of many reasons why they were being shunned. Surmising for months that their ex-communication would be inevitable, they had all but closed on the Atlas E site in Osage City, Kansas, which was now listed for only $55,000, an absolute bargain for 15,000 sq. ft. of hardened underground floor-space with additional above-ground concrete structures. The world-wide depression had caused the price of real-estate, especially in rural areas, to crater. Their offer of $40,000 was immediately accepted. The couple packed all of their belongs into a large trailer, hooked it up to their shiny new F-350 pickup, yet another reason they were being shunned, and headed off to Kansas to start a new life in the complete security of an abandoned missile silo.

CHAPTER 41

New Years in Bimini

December 31, 2065

The UN had tried desperately to shield the occupants of Bimini from the global bad news that was breaking daily in the world beyond their little chunk of paradise. The island's budget, which was designed to keep the islanders in a happy, reproductive state of mind, was seemingly infinite, at least for now. The UN still held out hope that the NoMs of Bimini would eventually start reproducing with each other, and create a viable pool of fertile, next-generation, non-mutated humans.

As the evening sun neared the horizon, Sally and Vicky headed down to the island's harbor-area for what was being promoted as an epic New Years' Eve bash. The best party that this all-party-all-the-time island had ever seen.

The two friends were looking forward to spending their final evening of 2065 dancing and partying to some oldies, but goodies, courtesy of the iconic super-star Taylor Swift, whom the UN was flying to the island to entertain the

NoMs as they welcomed the New Year. The singer may have just turned 76, but she was still in great shape, and her voice was better than ever.

"Come on! Hurry up, slow poke!" screamed Vicky, ten paces in front Sally.

"It's a private concert, and it doesn't start for an hour. What's the big rush?"

"What's the rush? It's Taylor Swift… she's a goddess! An icon! My mom and grandma practically raised me on her music. If I am not right there in front of the stage, three feet from her when she sings *Look What You Made Me Do*, I will literally die."

Sally finally gave in and broke into a gallop to catch up with Vicky. The stage had been assembled next to the harbor. The two friends settled into the front row, dead center, and began consuming adult beverages as they waited for the festivities to begin. They were soon joined by Ricky, who had been pursuing Sally since they'd arrived on the island. She, on the other hand, had never seen him as more than just a friend.

Taylor Swift's performance didn't disappoint. As twelve o'clock and the New Year approached, Taylor ended the concert with one of her all-time classics *Shake It Off*. At the stroke of midnight, everyone toasted with the finest champagne as a spectacular fireworks display lit up the pitch-black Caribbean sky. Sally looked over at Ricky's face, backlit by the fireworks. In that moment, after being away from her family for over a year, she finally felt a slight romantic urge. The music, the holiday celebration, the alcohol, it was all too much. Sally ran over to Ricky, threw her arms around his neck, screamed "Happy New Year", and leaned in to give him a big, wet, sloppy kiss.

The military radios crackled in the distance. The colonel's command was clear, *"Strelyat', kogda zakhochesh'"* which is Russian for, "Fire at will."

The Russian snipers started by picking off patrons on the fringes of the concert crowd, one by one. The hand-full of Bimini security guards were also part of the first round to be eliminated. The use of suppressors meant that the report of their American-made rifles blended perfectly with the fireworks, causing the initial shots to pass completely unnoticed by the crowd.

The Colonel then screamed *"Zazhigat' vse!"* into his radio. Seconds later, dozens of American M18 Claymore mines, flat-panel directional weapons embedded in the edge of the stage, exploded, riddling the bodies of hundreds of fans in the first twenty rows of the crowd with deadly shrapnel. Simultaneously, high-yield explosives in trash cans, scattered throughout the crowd, were detonated. In less than ten seconds, 90% of the residents of Bimini were fatally wounded.

The Russian snipers, dressed head-to-toe in black clothing and tactical vests, quickly picked off the few remaining survivors as they struggled to escape the chaos. Three minutes after the first shot was fired, their mission was complete, and executed to perfection. The Russian special forces units sprinted back to the beach and waded out to their black dinghies hidden in the mangroves a dozen meters off beach. The elite troops fired-up the dinghies' silent electric motors. The small boats disappeared quickly and quietly into the moon-less midnight mist where they were retrieved by a pair of Russian midget submarines, one-mile off shore.

CHAPTER 42

The Investigation

January 7, 2066

One week after the Bimini massacre, UN Secretary General Oyvind Knudsen was sitting in a meeting room on the island with an international team of investigators. They were all trying to determine what had happened.

Of the 1,183 adult NoMs on Bimini, 1,180 had been at the New Year's concert. All but ten of those attendees were now dead. The ten survivors were all in critical condition. The only uninjured adult NoMs were three residents who had decided to stay in their apartments, watching the festivities on closed circuit television. Even more devastating, all the babies had been killed by a thermo-baric explosive planted in the island's nursery.

The Secretary General questioned the team investigating the incident. "What do we know for certain? What can we tell the press?"

The Russian member the team, Nik Sakoroff, spoke up. "Tell them the truth! Tell them what I've been telling you ever since we got here. That all of the evidence clearly points to the Americans."

The other members of the team rolled their eyes in complete and total disagreement.

Nik Sakoroff was furious, "We have found over one thousand shell casings, and every one of them is U.S. Army standard issue. And all of those Claymore mines that were detonated? Every one of them was American! The fifty-two remotely activated improvised explosives in trash cans scattered throughout the crowd? Every one of them were fabricated in America! They were all U.S. Army High Explosive 81 mm M43A1 mortar shells. Those are the facts! How much more damn evidence do you need?"

"It's not that simple, Nik," Deputy Secretary Morgan Paul interjected. "You know that!"

"The hell it isn't that simple!" responded Sakoroff, now fuming. "If you don't want to reach any conclusions, that's fine. Give the press the facts and let the public come to their own conclusions."

"Mr. Sakoroff. There are a hell of a lot more facts here than the ones you have pointed out," Secretary Knudsen stated. "How about the fact that the Americans were the biggest supporters and investors in the *Bimini Project* from the very start? Why the hell would they sabotage the program after they funded it?"

"I don't know! Why don't you investigate and ask them?"

"Mr. Sakoroff, you know damn well that it's a piece of cake to buy those American weapons on the black market. On top of that, don't you find it a bit strange that we haven't found one finger print or unexplained fragment of DNA on any of this evidence? All the shell casings appear to have been acid-washed. Whoever pulled this off was very careful to leave behind no evidence what-so-ever."

The Russian campaign of misinformation and misdirection was extremely effective. Even after the UN's twelve-month investigation, no evidence was ever found that pointed to the Russians conclusively. In the end, the international team of detectives were unable to declare for certain who was to blame. However, due to the Russian's effective propaganda campaign, the worldwide consensus was that it had been a United States-led operation. Meanwhile, nearly all the identified non-mutated humans who were willing and capable of producing future generations of fertile humanity, were now dead. The future of the human race appeared to be a lost cause.

Over the next decade, this hopelessness drove massive increases in divorce, suicide, crime and unemployment. Why stay married if humanity was ending? Why waste time inventing anything? Why work? Why not just kill your neighbor and steal his stuff? Why live at all?

Year after year, the tensions between nations rose and international relationships disintegrated as treaties collapsed. The tensions between Russia and the U.S. continued to escalate. In August of 2075, NATO invaded and reclaimed the ethnic-Russian portion of Ukraine which had been "liberated" by Russia back in 2015.

CHAPTER 43

The Tri-Centennial

July 4th, 2076

It was America's 300th birthday. The Tri-Centennial anniversary of the signing of the Declaration of Independence.

It was a beautiful afternoon in Southern California. Dr. Steve LaMascus, a 40-year-old Geology professor at UCLA, and his wife Nancy, who was also a Geologist and a senior manager at NOAA, the National Oceanic and Atmospheric Administration, were sitting on the beach in Santa Monica. Their two children, Rachel and Alex, played in the surf as Steve and Nancy lounged on the beach soaking up far more melanoma-triggering UV rays than they probably should have.

Steve was thoroughly enjoying the holiday, "What a spectacular day! We live five miles from the beach, Nancy. Why on earth don't we do this more often?"

"Because we have too much other crap to do," replied his wife. "We shouldn't even be here today. The sink is full of dishes; I have a dozen performance appraisals that need to be written by Monday; and, you should be mowing that jungle in our backyard before we end up in HOA-prison."

Steve let out a long, painful sigh. "My dear, if those are our priorities, then our heads aren't screwed on straight. This, right here, lying on the beach, watching our kids play in the surf…this should be a *lot* higher on our priority list. Definitely above dishes and the lawn."

"I guess you're right." Nancy smiled at her husband and gave him a kiss.

Suddenly, they felt the sand under their beach towels rumble. Their fellow beachgoers also sensed the tremor. Most stopped in their tracks for a few moments, and then carried on with their holiday activities.

"What do you think that one was? A 5.5?" asked Steve.

"Depends how far away it was, but it felt more like a 6.0 to me," replied Nancy as they both dove for their smart phones and began furiously typing and swiping.

"I see readings from hundreds of seismometer stations, but they aren't time-synched yet." mumbled Steve.

"Same here. But it looks like it must have been fairly big."

Locating the epicenter of an earthquake works something like GPS, but backwards. A GPS receiver uses the signals coming from at least four satellites to determine the location of the GPS receiver. In the case of an earthquake, the data from multiple seismometer stations is used to triangulate on the epicenter of an earthquake. In both cases, it's all about timing and trigonometry.

In the case of GPS, the math is pretty simple. GPS satellites all send a signal at precisely the same time. The receiver in your car, in your phone, or in your watch, measures the time difference between when the signal from each satellite arrives, and uses trigonometry to determine the GPS receiver's position on the earth. GPS signals travel at the speed of light, so every nanosecond equals one foot of distance. A GPS receiver merely counts the nanoseconds, throws in a few corrections for Einstein's theory of general relativity, and does the math.

Finding the epicenter of an earthquake uses a similar process. One difference is that sound waves are used instead of radio waves, and, in some ways, it can be little more complicated. One problem is that sound waves don't always travel in a straight line. Sometimes they zig zag through the earth's crust. Another problem is that, while the speed of light is relatively constant, the speed of sound through the earth can vary significantly depending on the density of the rock through which it is traveling. The speed of sound through water is another variable. Finally, all the seismometers must be time synchronized very accurately.

California's abundant seismicity activity, combined with its robust scientific community, had resulted in the state being wired with over four hundred seismic stations. These stations immediately relay their data to the Southern California Seismic Data Center at Cal Tech where geologists, backed by banks of computers, interpret the raw data and then push it out to other governmental and academic users, utilities, and emergency management services. In parallel, the national Earthquake Information Center also runs its calculations on every major earthquake anywhere on the planet, and pushes its data to the National Oceanic and Atmospheric Administration (NOAA) Tsunami Warning Center in Palmer Alaska.

"My data's not making sense", Steve stated, somewhat perplexed. "It looks like a *very* shallow epicenter. And the data looks really weird."

"Mine too," replied Nancy. "It's crazy-shallow. Almost on the surface of the ocean floor! And it's roughly 170 miles off shore, due West of us."

"So, maybe it's a turbidite flow? Maybe a big chunk of the continental shelf broke off?" suggested Steve.

"That's not really what the data looks like. And the epicenter appears to be west of the Rodriguez Seamount, out on the abyssal plane. There aren't any big structures that could break off out there. This is *really* weird. Strangest looking earthquake plots that I've ever seen." Nancy replied.

Steve shook his head, "None of this makes sense. But, if the epicenter is really that shallow, then there could be a tsunami. Right? We need to head inland now, just to be safe."

Nancy yelled for the kids to get out of the ocean. Steve scooped up their towels and beach chairs with one hand as he called-up real time data from California's system of tsunami buoys with the smart-phone in his other hand. Station 46054, thirty-eight miles west of Santa Barbara and Station 46069, near Santa Rosa Island both were already showing some strange Tsunami-like activity, but it was always tricky trying to determine how deep-water readings would relate to a wave's eventual characteristics after it was amplified by the shallow coastal waters closer to shore.

Alex and Rachel complained all the way to the car, but eventually the family hit the road at a velocity well above the posted speed limit. The beach behind them was still crowded with families oblivious to the potential dangers building far off shore. The traffic heading *towards* the beach was still far heavier than the traffic in Steve's lanes heading *away* from the beach. Nancy started yelling out the window and waving her arms, trying to tell people to turn around and head inland. She knew it was a futile effort, but it seemed better than doing nothing.

They sped east on the 10 and then north on the 405. Steve switched on the car radio for breaking news and updates, but all they heard was "quake chat". A DJ was joking about the low-magnitude earthquake as he took calls from listeners all over the Los Angeles metropolitan area. Damage appeared to be limited to a few soup cans falling from grocery store shelves and a city full of freaked out pets.

"This doesn't sound bad at all," complained their son Alex. "Why did we have to leave? No one else was leaving."

A few seconds later each of their smart phones started bleating the NOAA tsunami warning.

Less than a minute after that, the same obnoxious pulsating tone interrupted the DJ on the radio.

"This is a message from the emergency broadcasting system… A Tsunami alert has been issued for the Pacific Coast from San Diego, north to Vandenberg Air Force Base. This includes the metropolitan areas of Santa Barbara, Ventura, Oxnard, Malibu, Los Angeles, Long Beach, San Clemente, Oceanside and San Diego. The Mexican cities of Tijuana and Ensenada may also be affected. At 11:07 a.m. Pacific Daylight Time, a series of ocean buoys off the California coast detected wave motion consistent with a possible tsunami moving towards the coast at approximately fifty miles per hour. The exact magnitude of the potential tsunami cannot be estimated at this time, however, all residents in the aforementioned areas are encouraged to move to higher ground as soon as possible. We now return you to your regularly scheduled programming."

"Watch out!" screamed Nancy as dozens of cars driving in the south-bound lanes of the 405, began making high speed U-turns through the grass median to join them in north-bound lanes. A Range Rover went up on two wheels as it exited the median, turned in front of the LaMascus family and almost flipped. Steve and Nancy's plan for seeking the high-ground, and relative safety of the Santa Monica Mountains had suddenly become a very popular thing to do.

"Wow!" exclaimed Steve, narrowly avoiding another collision. "This is going to be a disaster, even if it ends up being a false alarm. The government has just told fifteen million people to move to higher ground, and they want them to do it in less than sixty minutes? There's no way that this can happen!"

"Steve, look out!" A Dodge mini-van exited the median in a cloud of dust, side-swiped Steve's new Jeep, and sped down the shoulder of the interstate.

"He just hit you, Dad! And he didn't even stop! Aren't you going to call the cops?" screamed his daughter Rachel from the back seat.

"Rachel, I can assure you that, right now, the police have far more important things to worry about than a dent in my Jeep."

One hour later, they were stuck in traffic on the 405 at the Sepulveda Pass. But at least they were now well above the water level of any reasonable tsunami. Not moving, they were all glued to their smart phones, searching for the latest alerts, and listening to the radio. The AM station had switched to a helicopter pilot flying high over Manhattan Beach in Los Angeles.

"No one can get off the beaches, nothing is moving. PCH -- The Pacific Coast Highway -- is clogged, bumper to bumper. It's a total stand-still. Thousands of people appear to have abandoned their vehicles and are now attempting to walk or run, inland, on foot, which is making a bad problem even worse..." There was a brief silence.

"I'm now looking at the ocean. I've never seen anything like this. The water has receded by at least a quarter mile from where it was a few minutes ago. This doesn't look good." There was another long silence and then the pilot began to panic, "Oh, dear God! Here it comes. The wave... It's not really a wave... It looks more like a massive pile of water... It's enormous. It must be at least 500 feet tall. This could wipe out half the city."

Nancy was watching a live feed on her cell phone of a reporter who was standing on Redondo Beach. His camera man continued filming as the mammoth mountain of water approached from behind him. The reporter was no longer reporting. His eyes were closed and he was praying. The screen darkened as the ocean towered over him... And then the feed went to static.

Steve had been monitoring other seismographs on his cell phone. All over the world, undersea shocks were being sensed, many in places that made no geological sense whatsoever. Large tremors were indicated off the coasts of Miami, New York, Singapore, and Seoul. In the Pacific Ocean, there were epicenters off the coasts of Tokyo and Osaka, in the English Channel near the mouth of the River

Thames, in Lake Michigan 60 miles from Chicago, in the Atlantic near Rio de Janeiro, in the south pacific off the coasts of Sidney and Buenos Aires, in the Gulf of Mexico off the coast of Houston, off New Orleans, near the mouth of the Mississippi and another near the mouth of Tampa Bay.

Rachel began sobbing as she watched the helicopter video of the wave engulfing the still crowded beach that she had been playing on an hour ago. One minute these people were enjoying their holiday, the next minute they were being crushed under hundreds of feet of sea-water, hopelessly fighting for their lives. Their throats and lungs burning as they were filled with salt water.

The video-stream from another helicopter panned as the tsunami washed over the city of Los Angeles. The wave raced over the top of the Wilshire Grand sky scraper. At that point, the horrific magnitude of the disaster was obvious.

"It cleared the Wilshire! That means the wave is over 1,000 feet tall!" exclaimed Steve as everyone in the car lost their cell coverage. The car radio was now transmitting only static.

"How high are we right now?" asked Nancy.

Steve glanced at his GPS watch, "978 feet above sea level. That's not going to be high enough!"

Steve and Nancy surveyed the situation outside of their Jeep. They were in the Sepulveda pass. Rocky hills towered above them on both sides of the 405.

Steve pointed at the highest peak and shouted to his family. "Get out of the car! Take nothing with you, and climb like hell!"

Steve kept his family in front of him as they scrambled over jagged rocks and boulders on the hillside. They were fighting for every possible life-saving foot of altitude before the water arrived. Ten minutes into their climb they heard the roar of the approaching deadly wave.

Steve continued shepherding his family up the treacherous slope. "Don't look back. Keep climbing. We're going to beat this! You can do it! Don't stop! Go, go, go!"

The jagged rocks sliced into their arms and legs as they scrambled recklessly. They were leaving trails of blood behind them as their Jeep and the thousands of cars below them got smaller and smaller.

Then it hit. The deafening roar of the wave mixed with muffled, terrified screams. The debris-strewn waters rushed through the Sepulveda Pass. The LaMascus family continued their ascent as the deluge continued through the pass and into the valley below, inundating the cities of Sherman Oaks, Van Nuys and North Hollywood, killing several million more people. When the water finally stopped rising it was 300 feet above the now submerged 405. Fortunately for the LaMascus family the water was 100 feet below the point to which they had climbed to safety. They finally stopped their ascent and looked around them. They didn't see a soul on any of the peaks protruding from the churning water. The family of four sat on the rocky hillside, hugged each other, and cried.

A similar scene was repeated all over the world. A massive tsunami raced up the River Thames and wiped out London. The tsunami off Singapore leveled not just that city-state, but Kuala Lumpur and Jakarta as well. The one off the coast of New York City buried not only NYC and Long Island, but every city and town on that strip of the East Coast from Atlantic City to Providence Rhode Island.

The wave then surged in-land to destroy Philadelphia, and up the Hudson River, annihilating every city along the way, including Albany and Schenectady.

One-thousand-foot-tall tsunamis in the Gulf of Mexico easily swamped New Orleans, and Houston, and then sent a deadly wave traveling north, up the mighty Mississippi, drowning the cities of Baton Rouge, and Vicksburg, petering-out eighty miles south of Memphis.

CHAPTER 44

The White House

July 4, 2076

The President's Chief of Staff knocked once and sprinted into the Oval Office without waiting for permission.

"Mr. President, we need to get you to Andrews immediately." He grabbed the President by the arm and drug him outside.

"What's going on, Paul?" asked the President as they stumbled onto the South Lawn of the White House. Eight secret service agents quickly formed a perimeter around the president and began running with him.

"We have no idea, sir. It appears that undersea, coastal earthquakes are occurring all over the world. Most are occurring in places where there is no history of tectonic plate activity. Sir, there is a real possibility that Washington, D.C. will be flooded by a tsunami."

"What about Linda?"

"The first lady is already on Air Force One, waiting for us."

"A tsunami?" The president asked as he pointed in the general direction of the Lincoln Memorial, "What about the Tri-Centennial celebration? There must be close to a million people out there on the Mall!"

"Mr. President, we need to get you into the air now. Once that's accomplished, then we can worry about everyone else," replied his Chief of Staff as they sprinted towards Marine One. The VH-92 presidential helicopter, and two decoys, had just landed on the South Lawn. It would be used for the quick hop to Andrews Air Force Base.

"What about Congress?"

"It's a holiday, sir. So, it's difficult to contact all of them, we're trying. If any of them are still in D.C., we'll evacuate them to the bunker under the Green Briar resort in West Virginia until we have a better understanding of what the hell is going on. The congressmen who are spending the holiday back in their districts are, unfortunately, on their own."

"This isn't code name *Kanyon,* is it?" asked the president as he saluted the Marine guards at the door of Marine One and climbed the stairs.

As they sat down and buckled their seat belts the Chief of Staff whispered, "Mr. President. *Kanyon* is highly classified, we can only discuss it in a secure facility..."

"Damit, Paul. If this really is *Kanyon*, then we are facing far bigger problems than finding a damn cone of silence SCIF."

"Spin it up, let's get out of here!" Paul yelled at the military pilots who had Marine One off the lawn and in the air before the door was even fully secured. "Mr. President, *Kanyon*, if it exists, has to be delivered by a Status-6 torpedo, and that torpedo can only be launched from a Khabarovsk submarine. All of Russia's Khabarovsk subs are currently in port. We know this for certain. They haven't moved for 3 months. And we know exactly where all of their Status-6 torpedoes are."

"So. Maybe they built more?" The president was now stroking his chin. "*Kanyon* scares the crap out of me, Paul. Cruise missiles, ICBMs, bombers, I know that we can shoot most of them down. We've spent billions ringing our coastlines with anti-missile defense systems like THAAD, Patriot, magnetic rail guns, and high energy LASERS. With those defensive systems on our coast-lines, we can shoot down anything that comes flying our way. Those Status-6 torpedoes are huge, right?"

"As big as a barn door, sir, and not stealthy at all. Our coastal sonar systems should have seen them coming from hundreds of miles away. There is no way that they could have slipped through our defenses. On the other hand, we have detected several EMP's -- electromagnetic pulses -- which could be from nuclear explosions. Maybe the EMP levels were lower than we anticipated because the detonations were under water? Or maybe this isn't *Kanyon* at all. Maybe it's some new natural phenomenon that just happened to start ripping the earth's crust apart today."

"That doesn't seem likely. If we detected EMP's, then it almost has to be nuclear. And if it's nuclear, then it's probably the Russians. But how? We need to figure this out fast," replied the President. He gazed out the window of his helicopter as Air Force One came into view in the distance. The highly-modified 747 was sitting at the end of the runway, engines spinning, and ready to fly. Marine

One approached Andrews Air Force Base at full speed. It dropped out of the sky like a rock, and landed with a thud, right next to the mobile stairway leading to the door of Air Force One.

Along the coast of Alaska, and across the northern coast of Canada, the U.S. and Canadian Missile Defense Agencies had spent four hundred billion dollars constructing a protective shield of powerful radars and anti-missile defense systems. A string of Canadian radars and anti-missile-missile silos known as the *North Warning System* was located along Canada's Northern coast stretching from the Beaufort Sea to the Hudson Strait, watching for any Russian missiles flying over the North pole. Meanwhile, other U.S. and Canadian launch silos and radars stretched from Alaska's Bering Strait all the way down the Alaskan and Canada coasts to just north of Seattle, protecting against a missile strike from across the Pacific. All of these under-ground missile silos were considered indestructible, and the radars were heavily fortified. But, as they had done elsewhere, tremors off the Alaskan and U.S. West Coasts, and other tremors in the Northwest passage, created massive tsunamis which destroyed the early warning radars. The waves then drowned all of the Canadian and American interceptor missiles as they sat helplessly in their 'indestructible' silos.

CHAPTER 45

The Kremlin

**July 4, 2076**

"Our strategies are being executed at near-perfection!"

"Any indication that the Americans, know what is happening to them?"

"Nyet! They are clueless, as usual."

"But why is Washington still standing? It was supposed to be flattened with all of the other near-coastal cities."

"Da. This is a problem, comrade. We are working on it."

Half-buried in the mud at the bottom of Chesapeake Bay, approximately 90 miles south of Washington, D.C. near the mouth of the Potomac River -- not far from Tangier Island -- was a large object with black Russian lettering on it. The device had been placed there two months earlier by a Liberian-flagged fishing trawler which was indirectly owned by the Russian government, through a series of shell companies.

Deep within this large metal tube was a software-driven timer. Four years earlier, an exhausted Russian software engineer had mis-programmed this timer by 60 minutes due to his misinterpretation of U.S. time zone maps and day-light-savings-time laws. The software error had also been overlooked by Russia's less-than-stellar team of quality-control specialists. As a result, the timer hit zero, one hour later than it should have.

The process that followed, however, was identical to what had occurred an hour earlier within the 284 other pre-positioned *Kanyon* weapons which had already detonated off the coasts of the Earth's largest metropolitan areas.

The misprogrammed timer first opened several valves. These valves released the contents of three, large, highly pressurized CO_2 tanks into several huge balloons which quickly inflated. These balloons slowly lifted the *Kanyon* weapon out of the mud, raising it off the seafloor towards the ocean's surface, but it would never get there. A sensor in the weapon continuously computed *Kanyon's* depth below the surface by measuring the surrounding water pressure. The Russians had determined that the ideal detonation depth, the ignition point where the resulting tsunami would be maximized, was exactly half way between the ocean floor and the surface of the ocean. When that depth was reached, things started to get interesting.

The last tasked performed by *Kanyon's* timer electronics, before they were vaporized, was to initiate a conventional explosion which was directed inward by a spherical shaped charge mechanism. By shaping the blast, the pressure on a smaller sphere of highly-enriched Uranium isotope was greatly magnified. This shock-wave initiated an atomic fission chain-reaction within the enriched Uranium. The Uranium atoms began to split which released even more energy, along with more sub-atomic particles, which caused even more Uranium atoms to split, and so on. Inside the sphere of Uranium was another solid sphere of Plutonium and highly pressurized Tritium gas which boosted the power of the primary explosion even more.

But the real power of the *Kanyon* bomb, which had been mass-produced secretly by the Russians in defiance of several nuclear nonproliferation treaties, came from its secondary or *fusion* stage. The energy released by the primary explosion drove down a mechanism known as a pusher-tamper. The pusher-tamper compressed the material in the secondary stage through a process called radiation implosion. This tremendous pressure, combined with the x-ray energy from the first stage, caused the fusion fuel in the secondary stage, Lithium-6 deuteride, to release over 100 mega-tons of nasty, destructive energy through the process of nuclear fusion (the process of forcing two atoms to become one atom). Each *Kanyon* bomb was the equivalent of 10,000 Hiroshima bombs.

To make matters even worse, surrounding each of these bombs, the Russians had included a 17,000lb casing of Cobalt 59. As the 100 megaton *Kanyon* bomb exploded in sleepy Chesapeake Bay, it not only released enough energy to create a 1,300-foot-tall tsunami, it also released a potpourri of highly energetic radioactive particles. Many of these were high-energy neutrons which were absorbed by the harmless Cobalt 59. As those neutrons were sucked-up by the Cobalt 59, it was transformed it into the deadly, highly-radioactive Cobalt 60 isotope. The blast then mixed this deadly material with the seawater that was now hurtling up the Potomac River to destroy Washington and Baltimore, drowning millions of residents and the tourists who had come to D.C. to celebrate the Tri-Centennial. In a matter of minutes, the nation's monuments, treasures and leadership were crushed under a 1,000-foot wall of lethal, radioactive sea water. The deadly wave would then continue speeding west, only stopping when it slammed into the Allegany Mountains sixty miles inland.

Very few congressmen would make it to the perceived safety of the Green Briar bunker. Those who did, would drown. The bunker was designed to survive a nuclear blast. It was never meant to survive a thousand-foot-tall tsunami. Even in the unlikely event that victims could swim to safety, the radiation from the Cobalt 60 in the sea water would give them acute radiation sickness, killing them within a month or two.

CHAPTER 46

Air Force One

July 4, 2076

Air Force One rotated and went wheels up three minutes before the tsunami washed away Andrews Air Force Base and the rest of the D.C. metropolitan area. The President gasped and his wife Linda wept as they witnessed the devastation unfolding below them. The aging Boeing 747 barely cleared the incoming wave as it climbed into the safety of the summer sky.

"Paul!" the President screamed at his Chief of Staff. "I need some damn answers! What the hell is going on?"

The intelligence systems on Air Force One weren't quite as capable as the ones in the White House, but they were still pretty good. Considering that the White House no longer existed, the resources in this three-hundred-foot-long flying-tin-can would have to suffice.

"We're trying to determine the status of our Air Defense Systems, Mr. President. Unfortunately, nearly all of them were based on our coasts. It appears that every last one of them have been flooded. Ditto for all of our allies in the UK, Australia, Canada, Japan, and Korea. Even the Chinese had most of their Dong Neng-3 anti-ballistic missile systems fielded along their coast-lines. It seemed like the perfect location for them at the time. Unfortunately, now they are all submerged under a thousand feet of water."

"So, we're defenseless?" asked the president.

"We do have a few other defensive systems, but our best defenses are gone." Paul's concern grew even more intense as he scanned dozens of computer screens in the aircraft's situation room. "And now I see that we're sensing fairly high radiation levels. It seems to be coming from the water below us."

"So maybe this *was* caused by a *Kanyon* bomb after all?" The president frowned. "For that to be the case, the Russians must have launched dozens of them, maybe even hundreds. How could we have missed hundreds of Status-6 torpedoes coming at us? How could we have missed the dozens of the Russian subs that would have been required to launch them? Why the hell did we put all of our missile defense systems on the damn coast line?"

The usually calm and collected president was now red with fury.

"Get me the Russians on the phone, now!"

"We've already tried to contact them, sir. No one in Moscow is answering."

"Then get me the Russian ambassador at their embassy in D.C.!"

"Sir, all of the embassy buildings in D.C. are gone. I was told, however, that the Russian Ambassador and his family flew back to Moscow three days ago. They claimed that it was for some family event, like a wedding or something. In fact, it looks like virtually every senior Russian diplomat returned home over the past two weeks, for a variety of reasons. Nikolaev, Stepanov and Alexeev are the only three senior Russian officials who were still at the Russian embassy in Washington as of yesterday."

The president looked up in astonishment. "Those are our three double-agents! The Russians must have known about them all along." He buried his head in his hands. "So, all of that 'valuable, top-secret Russian information' that those three fed us over the past five years was just a pile of fake news that the Russians gave them to mislead us?"

The president got up from his chair and paced around the tiny airborne situation room, "What are our options, Paul?"

"The radioactive water will recede in a couple days, but tens of millions, maybe over one hundred million U.S. citizens, have already been killed. If this really is a result of *Kanyon* bombs, Cobalt 60 has a half-life of over 5 years, so the Atlantic, Pacific and Gulf coasts – and maybe up to a hundred miles inland -- are all going to be uninhabitable for decades.

The President, an engineer by training, sat down and started thinking out loud. "From what little I remember of my college physics and chemistry, Cobalt 60 is some nasty crap. The worst part is that human organs – the liver, kidneys, and bone-marrow – all soak up Cobalt 60 like crazy. And then, as it decays, it radiates into the surrounding tissues, resulting in cancer throughout the body. We will have to quarantine all of those coastal areas for at least a decade."

Paul shook his head. "That will be almost impossible. We can't control our border with Mexico. How are you going to stop looters from going into those coastal areas to steal things, only to have the radiation kill them? That's a boarder four times as long as the one we have with Mexico."

"I could care less about the looters. Serves them right. A bigger problem will be that those stolen, radiation-soaked products will be brought back into the uncontaminated areas and then resold. Normal commerce and trade could spread the radiation everywhere."

"The radiated areas do appear to be massive," added Paul. "Nearly 20% of the U.S. in terms of land mass, and probably 50% in terms of population."

"Didn't our intelligence agencies study this?" asked the president. "Didn't the CIA pay those two researchers, what were their names? Le Mehaute and Wang down at Rosenstiel? We had them model the effects of *Kanyon*-like weapons, right"

"The CIA didn't pay them directly, we funneled the money to them and several others through the U.S. Corp of Engineers. Their models all predicted that the waves could be around 1,000 feet tall, or even higher. That part appears to have been correct. But most of the models also predicted that the water would only travel a few miles inland. That part appears to have been way off."

"So, what the hell is happening? Why is the water traveling so far?"

Paul shrugged his shoulders, "Who knows. Maybe the bomb was bigger than they modeled, maybe their tests in a glorified bathtub didn't scale well to the real world. It's not like we allowed them to verify their models by exploding megaton bombs in the ocean."

The president tried to shake the cobwebs out of his head. "So, other than millions of dead Americans, our biggest immediate problem is that virtually all of our defensive missile systems are in those flooded radiation zones, and they are now useless. We have virtually no defensive options, which means that our only remaining option is offense. Right?"

The Chief of Staff stared at the ceiling of the aircraft in despair, "Mr. President. Are you asking me if we need to respond with an all-out nuclear attack?"

"Paul, I'm certainly open to any other options that you would like to suggest. Is there any other choice? Are our nuclear weapons ready?" asked the president.

"Yes, sir. All of our offensive assets are either in submarines, in missile silos in the Dakotas, or on B-21 Stealth bombers in Missouri. All of those weapons are safe under the sea, or high, and dry in the middle of the country."

"And the only other option would be to do nothing, and wait for the Russians to destroy our offensive weapons as well, right?"

"Yes, sir. We've war-gamed this thousands of times. At this point, your only move is to take out their nuclear missiles before they can take out yours."

The president shook his head and sighed, "God bless America. I have the biscuit here in my pocket. Get the codes from the football and let's launch everything that we have."

The launch order was sent from Air Force One to an E-6 "doomsday" TACAMO aircraft orbiting nearby. The TACAMO's five-mile-long dual-wire trailing antennas were already deployed, ready to re-transmit the encrypted launch order to NATO's strategic launch assets stationed all over the world via an ultra-secure, ultra-low-frequency radio waveform. The message was received by fourteen U.S. Ohio-Class, and four British Vangard-Class submarines scattered in oceans all over the planet. These eighteen massive, multi-billion-dollar submarines elevated themselves from their hiding spots in the ocean's murky depths, and rose to just a few meters below the surface. They opened their missile-tube hatches, and simultaneously released their hell. Over four-hundred UGM-133A Trident II ballistic missiles, each with fifteen warheads were now hurtling towards the Russian homeland.

CHAPTER 47

Meanwhile, Back at the Kremlin

July 4, 2076

"Da, comrade. Washington is gone, but the Americans appear to be launching their nuclear weapons. The President must have escaped in time to give the command. Or maybe NORAD just launched on their own, without waiting for an order. We never did fully understand their nuclear launch approval processes."

"It doesn't matter now. Launch our ICBMs immediately, and send a press release stating that Russia is responding to the United States' unprovoked nuclear attack on Russia. You are certain that our missile defense systems will stop these NATO missiles?"

"Da, comrade. That is what our war-game simulations indicate."

With NATO's shore-based missile defense systems submerged under hundreds of meters of radioactive water, the

Russian RS-28 SATAN 3 intercontinental ballistic missiles, armed with Avangard 15Yu71 hypersonic warheads, easily penetrated U.S. airspace and destroyed every American Missile silo. The B-21 bomber-base at Wittman AFB in central Missouri was also destroyed. In both cases, however, the Russians were too late. The Minuteman IV silos were empty – America's ground-based missiles had already been launched and were heading over the North Pole towards Moscow. Wittman's B-21 stealth bombers, likewise, were already on their way to attack the Russian homeland.

The destruction, however, was not limited to America's military bases. Other Russian missiles delivered megaton warheads to wipe out Earth's remaining major inland cities, those which had not already been destroyed by the coastal tsunamis -- cities like Phoenix, Denver, Mexico City, and Beijing.

For centuries, Russians had felt used, abused, and disrespected. The Russian people felt like they had done all the heavy-lifting to win World War II, but had received the short end of the stick in the aftermath. The USSR had been the first country to launch anything into orbit, and the first to send a man into space. After the U.S. Space Shuttle was retired, American astronauts had been forced to rent rides into space aboard Russian rockets, for nearly two decades, because the U.S. had no way to launch humans into space themselves. Still, the Russians got no respect from the rest of the world.

The genetic mutation issue had hit Russia especially hard. The Russian government had mandated aggressive genetic therapy for all of its citizens, giving them, essentially, a 100% compliance rate. NATO's bloody invasion to reclaim the "Russian portion" of the Ukraine, however, had been the final straw. If respect would not be given to Mother Russia, then she would take it by force.

The Russians could see that the world was falling apart around them. They were convinced that the solution for the humanity's problems was for Russia to finally take its rightful place as the world's sole super power. And Russian military officers had convinced Russia's political leaders that their plan was fool-proof.

Time and surprise are the most important weapons of war, and the Russian's war-plan had been designed to give them both. The tactic of using fishing trawlers to pre-place the *Kanyon* megaton bombs along the coastlines of the entire free world had been a brilliant idea. By doing this, the Russians achieved total surprise, eliminated all of their enemy's defensive missile systems, created total confusion, and virtually won the war before the rest of the world knew that a war had begun.

If Washington, D.C. and America's President had been wiped out in the first wave, as planned, the free world's ICBMs and strategic bombers may have never launched. The Russians would have destroyed them in their silos and hangers. The Russian generals, however, always had a back-up plan. Even though the United States and UK had launched their missiles in the nick of time, the Russian generals were confident that their defenses (which, unlike those of the U.S., were still in perfect working order) would shoot down most, if not all, of the incoming warheads.

Shooting down an InterContinental Ballistic Missile (ICBM) is no easy task. It has been compared to shooting a bullet out of the sky with another bullet. The easiest place to shoot down a missile is during its launch/boost phase, when the missile provides the biggest target (its engines are still burning, providing a large heat signature) and the missile is moving very slowly. Unfortunately, the boost phase usually occurs over the other guy's territory, and it usually occurs with no warning, so it is seldom practical to attack a missile during the boost phase. There are, however, methods to *detect* the boost phase, and to quickly compute the trajectory of the missile.

Several Russian military satellites were indeed flying over the various launch sites during the boost phase of the American and UK ICBMs. These Russian satellites quickly transmitted the probable trajectories of the warheads to Russia's so-called *hunter-killer* satellites, and also to their defensive systems back on Russian soil.

After the initial burn, an ICBM's boost-stage engines are jettisoned. The missile leaves Earth's atmosphere and enters the midcourse 'coast phase'. At this point an ICBM would be a sitting-duck for a space-based attack. This is also when the payload breaks apart and each missile deploys fifteen MIRVs (Multiple Independently-targetable Reentry Vehicles). Each U.S. MIRV is armed with a W80 thermonuclear warhead, which has its own guidance system and can be directed to attack a different city or target. Of equal importance, however, is that each ICBM also contains hundreds of MIRV *decoys*. These decoys are simple, cheap and very effective.

As they entered the vacuum of space each NATO ICBM deployed hundreds of metalized Mylar balloons – similar to grocery-store party balloons -- which, when inflated, had the same size, shape and radar cross-section as a real MIRV warhead.

Each balloon also included a tiny battery-powered EMI (radio frequency) generator which perfectly simulated the electrical noise that would emanate from a real warhead. In the vacuum of space, the balloons flew through the void at 15,000 mph, just like the warheads.

At this point, there were approximately 8,000 nuclear armed MIRV's and over 200,000 decoys, flying over the north pole, hurtling towards Russian soil. Obviously, there was no practical way for Russia to shoot expensive interceptor missiles at over 200,000 targets. Russia's only option was to use high-energy LASERS mounted on their space-based hunter-killer satellites. Each of Russia's 900 space-based LASERs should have been able to burn holes in one American MIRV or one decoy every five seconds. So, it should have been easy for Russia to destroy all 8,000 MIRVs and all 200,000 decoys during the 16-minute midcourse portion of the ICBMs' flight. That was the Russian Generals' fail-safe backup plan.

Contrary to their plan, however, none of the American warheads were even damaged. Unbeknownst to the Russians, the Americans had covered their MIRVs with a highly polished mirrored surface which reflected the energy from the powerful Russian LASERs harmlessly into space.

As the U.S. and British MIRVs re-entered the atmosphere over Russia, the decoy balloons burned up instantly. This gave Russia's Don 2NP / 5N20P radars a clear view of the 8,000 *real* MIRVs which were now veering off towards their preprogramed targets. The Don 2NP is a massive, electronically scanned radar system – It is the *eyes* of Russia's Samolet-M anti-missile system. Unfortunately for the Russians, the radar's software immediately crashed due to multiple stack overflows. The radar's trajectory prediction algorithms failed miserably as they tried in vain to track all 8,000 MIRVs streaking towards them.

The system had never been stress-tested to this level. The Samolet-M technicians weren't supposed to launch their A–235 Nudol anti-ballistic missiles until the Don 2NP radar had computed the intercept trajectories. The technicians could see on their screens that the warheads were getting closer. They could also see that the radar's fire-control-computer wasn't anywhere close to computing an answer.

"Dolzhny li my zapuskat' ili net?" (Should we launch or not?) asked the 22-year-old Lieutenant.

"My dolzhny nachat'. Yesli net, my vse umrem!" (We must launch. If not, we will all die!) replied his supervisor, a 24-year-old Captain.

The technicians each retrieved their launch keys, inserted them into their respective slots, they threw a series of switches, put their hands on the keys, looked at each other and counted: *"Odin, dva, tri, Zapusk!"*

Their keys turned, and two hundred A–235 Nudol anti-ballistic missiles headed into the gray, dreary, Russian sky.

Even if the radar software hadn't crashed, two hundred A-235's would have barely put a dent in the armada of 8,000 incoming MIRVs. Each A-235 was equipped with a small nuclear warhead which was designed to destroy a single MIRV, so a direct hit wasn't required, it only had to be close.

Years ago, the Russian weapon designers had decided to program the A-235's on-board software to detonate the nuclear warheads when the rockets ran out of fuel, even if they hadn't successfully intercepted an incoming MIRV. Their logic was that the world would be ending anyway, so maybe they'd get lucky. Maybe they would hit an incoming MIRV by accident.

The result was that the first two hundred nuclear blasts in the atmosphere above Russian soil were not from the West, but were Russia's own defensive nuclear devices detonating, hoping to 'get lucky'. Unfortunately for Russia, those defensive blasts did not destroy even one of the 8,000 incoming MIRVs. Seconds later the MIRVs found their targets, ignited their multi-stage thermonuclear weapons, and leveled, not just Moscow, but every significant city and military base in Mother Russia.

CHAPTER 48

After the Apocalypse

April 14, 2078

The nuclear exchange and nuclear tsunamis had killed 90% percent of the Earth's inhabitants. The electromagnetic pulses (EMPs) from the airborne nuclear blasts had knocked out all major power grids and destroyed most of the planet's semiconductor-based devices.

The overwhelming majority of humans who survived had no idea how to live without electricity, or without a nanny-state to provide for their every need. They had never lived off the land. Over the next three years, an additional 95% of that remaining 10% died from starvation, disease, or from radiation poisoning. And 98% of those survivors were infertile genetic mutants. The future of humanity did not look promising.

A glaring exception to those percentages were the communities of Mennonites scattered across the Central United States.

The Mennonite community near Paris, Missouri for instance was thriving. Shunning virtually all contact with the outside world had given them tremendous advantages:

- Since they had avoided the *Big Five* genetic enhancements, their population was 100% mutation-free, and they were reproducing like rabbits. They were the ideal NoM population.
- The Mennonites had also refused to be genetically tested and had declined participation in the Bimini project, thus avoiding the island's massacre of NoMs.
- Their choice to live in hardened bunkers, to protect themselves from the false threat of genetic spraying, ended up, coincidentally, protecting them from the nuclear blasts and fallout.
- Their paranoid habit of always having 6 months of emergency rations on-hand served them well in the aftermath of the nuclear exchange.
- Since they didn't trade with outsiders, they avoided the ill-effects of accidentally purchasing supplies stolen from highly radioactive areas.

For the first two months after the nuclear exchange, the Paris Mennonites didn't leave their bunker. One of their elders, Brother Mathew Bontrager, had been a nuclear reactor engineer at Missouri's Callaway nuclear plant, prior to joining the congregation. He knew that radioactive fallout posed the greatest threat during the first two weeks following the blast. The community, however, voted to remain underground for nearly two months as an added precaution.

Six months after the nuclear exchange, the Mennonite community began conducting expeditions in various directions to determine what had happened to neighboring areas. All the homes they came across were either empty, or the inhabitants were deceased.

The town of Paris, Missouri was empty. They searched the entire shoreline of Mark Twain Lake which was twenty miles to their east. They didn't find a single living soul. The towns of Madison, Holiday, Monroe City, Rowena, and even Hannibal, were all deserted ghost towns.

"We can't be the only survivors," exclaimed Samuel after returning from another unsuccessful expedition.

His sister Tessa chimed in, "Wouldn't it make sense to expand our search?"

"Why?" asked Vernon, the community's chief elder. "We are doing fine and dandy as we are. Our isolation has been the key to our survival. What good could possibly come from external entanglements?"

"We could find fellow Mennonites!" replied Tessa.

"Where? The Moberly and Pleasant View Mennonites already joined us years ago."

"No, Brother Vernon. Further than that. Much further. We could check on the Columbia Mennonite Mission, and then we could travel down to Bethel Missouri, Oak Ridge, our Brothers and Sisters in Warrensburg, the Sycamore Grove Mennonites. Then we could venture even further to check on the Lyndon, Kansas Mennonites."

"Ah! Lyndon, Kansas! That's just a couple miles from Osage, Kansas, isn't it?" Vernon quipped.

"Exactly!" replied Samuel, "We may also pay a visit to Sister Jane and Brother Joseph at the Atlas E facility outside of Osage. What is so wrong with checking-in on our grandparents while also surveying our other Mennonite communities?"

"Your grandparents were shunned a decade ago. They left us. They are no longer your family. What do your father and mother think of this frivolous escapade?" asked the elder, looking over at Sarah and her husband Jonah. "Are you in favor of this foolishness? Will you be joining them? Who will watch their children?"

Sarah thought for a moment before she responded, "Jonah and I have no intention of joining them, but an expedition to search the lands to our west certainly isn't a bad idea. They are young and strong. We will watch their children while they are gone. At their age, such an adventure will build character. Our community is growing. Surely God's destiny is for us to spread beyond this compound, at some point, to repopulate the earth. Would not this be a right and proper way to start?"

Brother Vernon was not impressed. "It will be a long journey. What will you need in the way of supplies?"

"Three horses, two wagons, and rations for sixty days," answered Samuel. "The round trip will be roughly four hundred miles. If we plan to travel every other day, and average twenty miles on those travel-days, then we should be gone for around forty days. Taking enough supplies for sixty days should give us plenty of margin."

CHAPTER 49

The Trek

May 20, 2078

The adventurous group of young-adult Mennonites consisted of Jane's grandson Samuel, his sister Tessa, and eight of their friends. They had been trudging through the Ozark Mountains and over the Great Plains of Missouri and Kansas for thirteen days. Along the way, they had hop-scotched from one Mennonite community to the next. Many of those communities, sharing the Paris community's fear of aerial genetic spraying, had dug underground shelters for protection. Those shelters had protected many of them from the nuclear exchange, and those communities were now thriving.

Others, like the Mennonites of Warrensburg, Missouri, had been annihilated when neighboring Whitman Air Force Base, home to America's stealth bomber fleet, had been flattened with multiple 10 megaton explosions. No shelter could protect humans from a nearby blast of that magnitude.

The non-Mennonite towns all appeared to be uninhabited -- except for countless human skeletons which were picked clean by the few remaining birds. The fact that the attack had occurred on the biggest national holiday of the century meant that virtually everyone had been outside and fully exposed to the deadly radiation blasts. Now, however, as the group trudged through the state of Kansas, the destruction appeared to be less severe than it had been around Whitman.

The Mennonites were still a devoutly religious order, but ever since the nuclear exchange, many of them, the youth in particular, had become a bit more edgy and jaded. At nineteen years of age, Jeb was the second youngest member of the group. He was also the most jaded of them all.

"Hey Isiah," Jeb screamed at his friend walking on the other side of the group, "How many Pollocks does it take to screw in a light bulb?"

"Jebhidia Van Deterwalt! Watch your language" screamed Ruth, who, at twenty-six years of age, was one of the more conservative members of the bunch.

"Sorry, Mom!" joked Jeb, knowing how much Ruth hated it when her peers mocked her for being a stodgy old maid.

Isiah replied sarcastically to his friend, "I have a keen thirst for knowledge oh Brother Jeb, so please enlighten me. Precisely how many Pollocks *does* it take to screw in a light bulb?"

"None. Because it's the Apocalypse. There are no more light bulbs and there's no Poland either!"

The party groaned at Jeb's lame attempt at humor, but they appreciated his efforts to keep their spirits up.

"Thank you, thank you!" responded Jeb, taking a bow of gratitude to no one in particular. "I can make end-of-the-world jokes like there's no tomorrow!"

"Such poor taste," mumbled Ruth, shaking her head.

Isiah suddenly snapped to attention and pointed to his left.

"Look! Is that smoke coming from the chimney of that concrete structure?"

Jeb squinted and used his hand to shade his face from the sun. "Yes! That's smoke! Someone must be in there!"

———◦◦◦———

Jane sat at her desk and began writing in her journal as tears dripped onto the pages. She was seventy-two years old, but she felt the pains of age well beyond her years. The fact that no human lifeform was left to read her journal made her grief even more unbearable.

When the blast came a year and a half ago, Jane had been down in the hardened silo while her husband, Joseph, had been up top, tending to their crops. When the Russian thermonuclear devices detonated over Kansas City and Whitman, the resulting Gamma rays, high energy protons, neutrons, and x-rays, swept across the plains and ripped through Joseph's aging body like a meat saw through the carcass of a heifer.

Joseph had managed to stumble back into the hardened silo before the shock wave hit, so he had survived. His entire body, however, was covered with radiation burns. Internally, his organs were scarred even worse.

All the communities around them had been leveled by the blasts. Jane had waited four weeks for the radiation to subside before she ventured out. She had traveled several miles in each direction. She found nothing but death and total devastation.

Jane was a medical doctor and had collected a sizeable stash of drugs and medical equipment in the silo. She knew, however, that the chances of saving Joseph's life were slim. After a year and a half of excruciating pain, Joseph had finally succumbed to his injuries.

"I believe that I am the last person alive on the Earth" she wrote. *"This appears to be the culmination of humanity. This is how it all ends. Exactly as T.S. Eliot predicted. Not with a bang, but with a lonely, pathetic whimper… and I am, at least partly, to blame – Dr. Jane Stewart."*

She heard a noise outside. What could it be? Was it the wind? A pack of wolves?

Jane put down her pen, scrambled up the steps of the bunker as fast as her frail 72-year-old legs could carry her and grabbed her double-barrel 12-gauge shot-gun. She then walked towards the small window and slowly opened the heavy blast-shutters for a glimpse outside.

About a football field away from Jane's bunker, the group of young Mennonites were approaching.

"Someone is inside!" screamed Isiah. "And they're pointing a damn 12-gauge at us!"

Jeb commanded the horses to stop, and the entire group quickly huddled behind the wagons for cover.

Isiah shouted, *"Don't shoot! We mean no harm!"*

———————————

Jane peeked out the window. Her aging ears heard a voice scream something like: *"Shoot. Burn the farm!"* Jane couldn't see squat. She pointed her shotgun in the general direction of the unidentified noise.

Jane's head was spinning. She faced the classical choice of fight or flight, neither of which sounded appealing at her advanced age. There were no good options. So, she did the only thing that seemed to make sense at the time. She fired two warning shots into the air, reloaded, and yelled "Get off my damn property! Go away! Now!"

———————————

Tessa looked over at her brother Samuel in shock, "Um, is that our grandmother?"

"It's been a long time, but it sure sounds like her."

"It definitely sounds crabby enough to be her! And it's absolutely her style to shoot first and ask questions later!" exclaimed Tessa, now laughing.

"I think that we are fairly close to Osage City, so I guess that this *could* be the Atlas E site," stated Samuel. "It's kind of hard to tell when 95% of the structure is buried underground."

"Grandma Jane, is that you?" yelled Tessa.

Jane had lost her glasses months ago, and was blind as a bat without them. Her hearing wasn't much better than her eyesight, but she could've sworn she heard a voice say the words "Grandma Jane." With tears welling-up in her eyes she put down her shot-gun and ran towards the bunker door.

CHAPTER 50

The Epilogue

OK, I'm tired of writing. You all can fill in the rest of the story from here. The Mennonites, or the Amish, or the Mormons, or whoever best resists the "curse of CRISPR" ends up surviving and repopulating the planet, and they all live happily ever after. The end.

The promise of CRISPR is so incredible...

And access to CRISPR kits is so universal, and so easy, and so cheap...

And the risk of something unforeseen going wrong is so certain...

That there really is almost no way that a scenario like the one in this novel *won't* happen.

You can nit-pick our little book to death if you like:

For instance, many of the genetic mutations which (in the book) are accomplished in childhood via vaccinations, or through the water supply, or by aerial spraying, would probably have to be done in-vitro – at least for now (for reasons too complicated to discuss here).

But this doesn't mean that all of those events won't happen; it only means that those things may take *slightly* longer to come to fruition than they do in this novel.

To keep things interesting, we tried to make everything occur in the lifetime of the main character, Jane. And we designed the plot so that Jane would be involved in as many of those steps as practical.

Obviously, no single person is going to dominate every aspect of the CRISPR field like Jane does. In reality, there are going to be tens of thousands of "Janes".

There are other things to nit-pick. The 405, for instance, has a concrete wall in the median, not a grass median where those people were making emergency U-turns to escape the tsunami. But didn't those crazy U-turns make the story more exciting?

Around ten years ago, I read *NEXT*, the last novel that Michael Crichton wrote before his untimely death. I was always a huge Michael Crichton fan. He was brilliant. And his novels, although fiction, were well-researched and, generally, scientifically accurate.

He never sucked you into a fantastic, unbelievable scenario, only to explain it away later as a dream-sequence, or interplanetary aliens, or whatever. He almost always had a sound scientific basis for his seemingly impossible scenarios.

But while reading Crichton's dystopian techno-thriller, *NEXT*, I was a little disappointed. As with *CRISPR*, the plot of *NEXT* revolved around DNA and its manipulation, but *NEXT* also explored other important questions like:

Who owns your DNA? If a company takes your DNA and modifies it, do you still own it, or does the company own it?

If a company discovers that you have an amazing, unique gene -- one that cures cancer, for instance -- do you own the rights to that gene, or does the company who did the work to discover that trait, own "your" gene?

Those plot points were great, but what bugged me was how he glossed-over how hard it was (back in the early 2000's) to manipulate human DNA. In Crichton's novel, several huge, multi-billion-dollar genetic labs create some incredible gene manipulations, which I found implausible (on the par with aliens and dream sequences).

Today, however, with 20-20 hind-sight, it looks like Mr. Crichton may have massively *underestimated* the future. With CRISPR technology, many of his "impossible" DNA modifications -- the ones that were so unbelievable to me at the time -- may soon be performed by a high school sophomore in her parent's garage using a CRISPR kit that she bought on the internet with her left-over lunch money.

An incomplete set of references and acknowledgements

"Stealing an idea from one person is called plagiarism – but stealing ideas from many people is considered research." -- Unknown

We used many scientific and news sources for this novel. A few of them are listed below. Just because they are listed does not necessarily mean that the original authors agree with the contents of this book, or how we interpreted (or misinterpreted) their research, writings and/or ideas.

In many cases, we had to greatly oversimplify processes to avoid boring the reader, but we tried to avoid taking artistic license with any key facts.

One question that some readers had was: *When scientists discover that the "Big Five" artificial genetic changes are causing sterility, why don't they just use CRISPR to undo all the changes? Or, better yet, why don't they create a genetic modification that fixes the sterility issue?*

We hinted at a few reasons for why no one could genetically reverse the sterility issue. For one, the power of gene drive is very scary. Gene drive could, conceivably, prevent a fix from "taking".

One of our editors, Steve LaMascus, suggested that a more likely scenario would be if the Big Five mutations inadvertently caused the formation of a Prion (as in mad cow disease) that would then impact haploid cells in the second and third generations.

The point is that there are thousands of ways that things can (and will) run amuck with CRISPR technology. For this book, we choose a compelling set of scenarios which just happens to result in the most interesting novel ever written in the history of literature.

Please feel free to do more research at the following sites:

Chapter 1

http://www.realclear.com/living/2016/01/08/buy a former government missile silo and live the doomsday dream 12655.html#ixzz 4cMYUZ1Mz

Chapter 2

https://fitnessgenes.com/blog/finnish-skier-eero-mantyranta-and-his-favourable-genetics/
https://en.wikipedia.org/wiki/Eero_M%C3%A4ntyranta
http://www.hematology.org/About/History/50-Years/1532.aspx

Chapter 3

https://www.technologyreview.com/s/600774/top-us-intelligence-official-calls-gene-editing-a-wmd-threat/

https://geneticliteracyproject.org/2016/05/25/
    can-crispr-make-cheap-gm-based-wmds/
http://www.cnn.com/2016/09/15/politics/john-brennan-cia-
    communist-vote/index.html
https://spectator.org/confirmed-john-brennan-colluded-
    with-foreign-spies-to-defeat-trump/
https://scifglobal.com/scif-definition-what-is-a-scif/
https://www.dni.gov/index.php/newsroom/congressional-
    testimonies/item/1757-statement-for-the-record-
    worldwide-threat-assessment-of-the-u-s-intelligence-
    community-before-the-ssci
http://blog.addgene.org/cpf1-update-comparison-to-cas9-
    and-ngago

Chapter 4

https://www.shmoop.com/gene-regulation-protein-
    synthesis/transcription-replication-similarities.html
http://www2.fiu.edu/~kavallie/F12CHM1033
    Ch11112112.pdf

Chapter 5

http://rna.berkeley.edu/crispr.html
https://www.vox.com/2017/10/25/16527370/
    crispr-gene-editing-harvard-mit-broad
https://zageno.com

Chapter 6

http://www.thenewatlantis.com/publications/
    the-truth-about-ddt-and-silent-spring

http://www.discoverthenetworks.org/viewSubCategory.asp?id=1259

https://en.wikipedia.org/wiki/Gene_drive

Chapter 7

https://globalnews.ca/news/1609753/study-shows-chicken-size-quadruples-in-60-years/

Chapter 8

https://www.technologyreview.com/s/409654/fuel-from-algae/

Chapter 9

https://www.greekmythology.com/Myths/Heroes/Bellerophon/bellerophon.html

http://www.ishr.org/countries/peoples-republic-of-china/organ-harvesting/

https://www.wired.com/2017/01/first-human-pig-chimera-step-toward-custom-organs/

Chapter 10

http://articles.extension.org/pages/26635/switchgrass-panicum-virgatum-for-biofuel-production

https://www.scientificamerican.com/article/the-ogallala-aquifer/

Chapter 11

https://www.ncbi.nlm.nih.gov/gene?Db=gene
&Cmd=DetailsSearch&Term=5187
https://en.wikipedia.org/wiki/PER1

Chapter 12

https://www.amazon.com/Machine-Make-Future-Biotech-
Chronicles/dp/0691126143

Chapter 13

https://ghr.nlm.nih.gov/gene/MSTN
https://en.wikipedia.org/wiki/Myostatin
http://www.nbcnews.com/id/5278028/ns/health-
genetics/t/genetic-mutationturns-tot-superboy/#.
WflHKWhSwRk
https://www.forbes.com/forbes/welcome/?toURL=https://
www.forbes.com/sites/paulrodgers/2014/01/27/
stone-age-hunter-had-blue-eyes-and-dark-
african-skin/&refURL=https://www.google.
com/&referrer=https://www.google.com/
http://www.independent.co.uk/news/science/how-one-
ancestor-helped-turn-our-brown-eyes-blue-776170.
html

Chapter 15

http://fortune.com/author/erika-fry/

Chapter 16

https://en.wikipedia.org/wiki/Jesse_Gelsinger
https://www.sciencedaily.com/releases/2008/08/080807175438.htm

Chapter 17

http://genetics.thetech.org/original_news/news60

Chapter 18

http://www.dramabookshop.com/photograph-51-anna-ziegler-starring-nicole-kidman
https://www.nytimes.com/2017/05/22/science/52-genes-human-intelligence.html
https://www.sciencenews.org/article/40-more-intelligence-genes-found
http://www.npr.org/2011/01/23/132737060/meet-william-james-sidis-the-smartest-guy-ever

Chapter 19

https://aiimpacts.org/brain-performance-in-flops/
http://www.npr.org/sections/money/2015/05/19/407736307/robots-are-really-bad-at-folding-towels

Chapter 21

https://bioviva-science.com/blog/2017/3/2/first-gene-therapy-successful-against-human-aging

Chapter 22

https://www.theguardian.com/science/2017/jan/26/first-
human-pig-chimera-created-in-milestone-study

Chapter 24

https://www.ncbi.nlm.nih.gov/pmc/articles/
PMC1771333/
http://www.slate.com/articles/health_and_science
/chromosomes/features/2012/blogging_the_human
genome/blogging_the_human_genome_elizabeth
_taylor_s_double_eyelashes_.html

Chapter 25

https://en.wikipedia.org/wiki/Stauffer_Mennonite

Chapter 29

http://beta.latimes.com/world/africa/la-fg-south-sudan-
child-marriage-snap-story.html
https://unmiss.unmissions.org/high-bride-prices-behind-
cattle-rustling-terekeka

Chapter 31

http://www.missilebases.com/communications-bunker-
paris-mo
http://www.atlasmissilesilo.com/atlas_e.htm
http://www.missilebases.com/osage-city-ks-atlas-e-site

Chapter 32

https://timeline.com/north-korea-poplar-tree-bcee4d72332f

https://www.nytimes.com/2017/11/04/world/asia/north-korea-south-korea-demilitarized-zone-tunnel-tourism.html

Chapter 34

https://www.balldrop.com/new-years-eve-marriott-marquis-times-square

Chapter 35

https://www.bahamas.com/islands/bimini

Chapter 40

https://en.wikipedia.org/wiki/Shunning

Chapter 41

https://fas.org/man/dod-101/sys/land/m18-claymore.htm

Chapter 42

https://en.wikipedia.org/wiki/M1_mortar

Chapter 43

http://geology.com/records/biggest-tsunami.shtml

Chapter 44

http://allnewspipeline.com/Nuclear Tsunami Nightmare.php

https://thebarentsobserver.com/en/security/2016/12/did-russia-test-doomsday-weapon-arctic-waters

http://www.popularmechanics.com/military/weapons/a24216/pentagon-confirm-russia-submarine-nuke/

http://freebeacon.com/national-security/russia-tests-nuclear-capable-drone-sub/

Chapter 45

https://edwardmd.wordpress.com/2013/06/15/teller-ulam-hydrogen-bomb/

http://nationalinterest.org/blog/the-buzz/americas-lethal-new-b-21-vs-the-b-2-stealth-bomber-15352

https://motherboard.vice.com/en_us/article/evpbzj/scientists-tell-us-what-would-happen-if-north-korea-detonated-a-hydrogen-bomb-underwater

Chapter 46

https://fas.org/nuke/guide/usa/c3i/e-6.htm

Chapter 47

https://www.thesun.co.uk/news/2066898/russias-satan-2-nuclear-missiles-rs-28-sarmat-warheads-uk/

https://nnsa.energy.gov/sites/default/files/nnsa/factsheet/w80-4_lep_final_edited.pdf

https://en.wikipedia.org/wiki/Don-2N_radar

https://www.rbth.com/defence/2016/06/23/russia-successfully-tests-new-missile-for-defense-system-near-moscow_605711

Chapter 48

https://www.ameren.com/missouri/callaway/nuclear-energy-at-callaway
https://en.wikipedia.org/wiki/Mark_Twain_Lake

Chapter 50

http://www.nytimes.com/2006/11/28/books/28masl.html

CPSIA information can be obtained
at www.ICGtesting.com
Printed in the USA
FSHW011556110920
73713FS